Best Wishes

[signature]

1

SHACKLETON BLISTER
THE PRICE OF JUSTICE

PHILIP CAINE

SHACKLETON BLISTER
THE PRICE OF JUSTICE

First paperback edition printed 2019 in the United Kingdom

ISBN 9780993374876

Published by REDOAK
www.philipcaine.com
For more copies of this book, please use the website above.

Critique & Editing: Gillian Ogilvie
Technical Editor: Malcolm Caine

Cover Design: www.gonzodesign.co.uk

Printed in Great Britain:
www.print2demand.co.uk

www.philipcaine.com

ABOUT THE AUTHOR

Philip's career began in hotel management and then transitioned to offshore North Sea, where he worked the boom years on Oil Rigs, Barges & Platforms. Seventeen years passed, and Philip returned to onshore projects taking a three year contract to manage accommodation bases in North & West Africa.

From Africa, Philip moved to the 'Former Soviet Union' where he directed multiple projects in Kazakhstan & Russia, a particularly exciting seven years where dealings with the KGB were an everyday event.

The end of the Iraq War in 2003 took Philip to Baghdad where, as Operations Director, he controlled the operations & management of multiple accommodation bases for the American Coalition. He left Baghdad in 2010. The last three years of his career were spent running a couple of support services companies in Dubai.

Philip's life experiences and time in Asia and the Middle East are the inspiration for his thrillers.

Also, by Philip Caine

'The Jack Castle Series'

PICNIC IN IRAQ

TO CATCH A FOX

BREAKFAST IN BEIRUT

THE HOLLOW PRESIDENT

AMERICAN RONIN

POSEIDONS RANSOM

SILK ROADS

SHACKLETON BLISTER
THE PRICE OF JUSTICE

Prologue

Spring 2013
Courtroom 4, The Old Bailey, London

The Court Usher's voice echoed across the big room. 'Will the defendant please rise.'

All eyes turned to the man standing in the dock, a few murmurs from the public gallery.

'Quiet please,' continued the Usher.

Justice Helen Wentworth took a sip of water, then removed her spectacles. For several seconds she looked at the standing man, then replaced her glasses and picked up a sheet of paper.

'This is a particularly sad case. Unhappily, the real sentence will be yours to bear for the rest of your life . . . Knowing you contributed to the death of your wife and unborn child, will haunt you until the day you die. That said, English Common Law demands you must be punished for your part in this tragic affair, and it is with some regret, I am bound to impose a suitable sentence. Your to-date impeccable record as a Police Officer, and the absence of any prior convictions, has been taken into consideration. Nevertheless, it has been found you were under the influence of alcohol, albeit marginally, when the accident occurred, resulting in the death of your family. Robert Anthony Stone, I therefore sentence you to four years imprisonment. I hope you may find the strength to live with the result of your actions. Take him down.'

Chapter One
Summer 2017
North Quay Offices, Manchester

The sign on the door read, *SHACKLETON BLISTER.
Confidential Enquiries*. The woman looked at the sign for
a few moments, then knocked. No answer. She knocked
again, turned the handle and entered. 'Hello?' Still no
answer.

Then, from the inner office, a man's voice. 'Hang on,
please.'

The woman looked around the room. A desk and chair,
with a small sofa in front. On the desk a laptop; a black
eyepatch lay on the keyboard. A bulb flickered in an old
desk lamp. In the corner, a filing cabinet; an open delivery
box with the remains of a pizza on top. The window was
open and the view across the waters of Salford Quays was
pleasant. The in-coming fresh air didn't quite mask the
faint smell of whisky.

A man entered.

She looked him up and down. 'Sorry to wake you. I did
knock.'

He ran his fingers through uncombed hair. 'Err . . .
yeah, sorry. Was a long night. Just catching up on a little
sleep.'

'Yes, quite. May I sit?'

He went to the desk, picked up the eyepatch and
slipped it on. 'Oh, yeah, sure . . . Miss?'

She noticed the scars on his hands and neck. 'Lang . . .
Amanda Lang.'

'Shackleton Blister.' He caught her slight smile. 'Yeah, it usually brings that response.'

'Oh, excuse me. It is a rather distinct nom de guerre.'

'And what's that supposed to mean?'

'Nom de guerre is . . .'

'I know the expression. I meant you using it.'

She smiled and eased back into the sofa. 'Shackleton Blister is not your real name. I know you began using it after you left prison.'

'Oh, yeah.'

'I also do not believe you were responsible for the death of your family.'

'Okay, lady. Who the hell are you, and what do you want?'

'As I said, my name is Amanda Lang, and I'm a freelance journalist.'

'Sorry. I don't talk to journalists.'

'Hear me out, please.'

'You got two minutes. What do you want?'

'What I want, is to help you bring the people responsible for the loss of your career, the death of your wife and child, and your subsequent imprisonment, to justice.'

'All that's behind me, love. There's no way you can change what happened. So, I think you'd better leave, Miss Lang.'

'Please, call me Amanda.'

He looked at her. Mid-thirties. Confident; well-dressed; attractive. Probably a strong character. Not from Manchester; the hint of a Scottish accent. He adjusted the eyepatch, then stood and went to the window. As he stared out across the Quays, he said, 'Why?'

'Why what?'

He turned and looked at her for several seconds. 'Why would you want to help me?'

'Because, Mister Blister I . . .'

'Call me Shack.'

She stood and joined him at the window. She frowned a little as she caught the smell of whisky on him.

'Because, Shack, I believe the people responsible for your situation, were also responsible for the death of my partner.'

Chapter Two
'She Likes You'

The trendy coffee shop, overlooking Salford's North Quay, was busy as usual. Shackleton was a regular.

The young waitress smiled as he approached. 'Morning,' she said, the thick Polish accent evident.

He gave a half-hearted smile. 'Mornin.'

A couple of people stood up from an outside table. 'This'll do,' he said.

The waitress nodded and began clearing the plates. 'How are you today? The usual?'

He sat down. 'I'm fine thanks. Yeah, tea and a bacon sandwich.'

The girl smiled. 'White bread, no sauce,' then turned to Amanda. 'Menus are on the table, Miss.'

'Oh, just a cappuccino for me, please.'

'Yes, Miss.'

As the waitress walked away, Amanda said, 'She likes you.'

'What?'

'Our waitress. She likes you, Shack. Though I can't see why.'

He frowned then turned and looked out across the water. 'You wanted to talk outside my office. Why?'

The girl returned with their drinks. She smiled at him. 'Bacon sandwich in two minutes.'

Shack turned to her. 'Cheers, love.'

As she walked away, Amanda said, 'There now. That wasn't too hard was it?'

'What?'

'Being pleasant to her.'

He sipped the steaming tea. 'What the hell do you want, lady?'

'I didn't want to talk in your office because I don't know how secure it is.'

He frowned. 'No one is gonna bug my place. I'm not that important.'

'It also smells a little.'

'Bacon sandwich, no sauce. I told chef to put extra bacon.'

Shack smiled. 'Thank you, Maria.'

Maria smiled at the use of her name. 'Let me know if I can get you anything else.'

As the girl went back inside, Amanda grinned. 'Extra bacon? Oh, yes, she likes you.'

He picked up the sandwich and munched into the soft white bread. 'Hmmm.'

She moved her chair a little closer to him, picked up her mug, took a couple of sips, then said, 'Have you ever heard of a government project called Overwatch?'

He shook his head. A small piece of crispy bacon fell to the plate.

'Overwatch was set up four years ago. A Home Office initiative to investigate police corruption, at the highest level, across the UK.'

He swallowed. 'Never heard of it.'

'Exactly. It was essentially a covert mission, with operatives reporting directly to the Home Secretary's office. Even the Police Commissioner knew nothing about it.'

'So how come, if it's that secret, you know about it, Mandy?'

She frowned. 'Because my partner, Sam, was part of Overwatch.'

Shack put the sandwich down and picked up his mug. 'And now he's dead.'

Amanda looked out across the sparkling waters of North Quay. 'She . . . she's dead.'

'I'm sorry. Can I ask what happened?'

Amanda, took another drink, then looked him in the eye. 'She was killed in an alleyway in London.'

'Sounds brutal. I really am sorry.'

For the first time since their meeting began, she felt the rough-looking guy in front of her did mean what he said. 'Thank you, Shack.'

'Can you talk about it?'

'It wasn't a random killing. She was murdered. She'd gone to a nightclub. I'd spoken with her earlier that evening. She said she was following some target and had no idea when she'd be home. There was CCTV footage of her leaving the club with a guy. The police report said she'd picked up a man in the bar and gone out to the alleyway, perhaps for sex or drugs. A chance encounter that had tragic consequences.'

He saw the tears well up in her eyes. 'That's enough, you don't need to go any further.'

'No it's fine. There's no way she would be interested in sex or drugs. They fabricated a reason for killing . . . murdering her.'

'Bastards,' he said quietly. 'Oh, sorry!'

She grinned at the profanity. 'No that's fine.'

He smiled. 'Do you want another coffee?'

16

She nodded. 'Okay.' *He has a nice face when he smiles*, she thought.

He waved to Maria. 'Another coffee and tea, please.' Then he turned back to Amanda. 'So, what do you want with me, lady?' He smiled again.

The humour in his voice when he said, 'lady,' was not lost on her. 'You can call me Amanda.'

The waitress put their drinks down and picked up the empty mugs. 'Can I get you anything else?'

He shook his head. 'Thanks, love.'

They both drank, then Amanda said, 'I want you to help me get justice for Samantha's and Christine's deaths.'

He adjusted the eyepatch. 'Chrissy . . . I always called my wife, Chrissy. You know, the price of justice can be very high, Amanda. And I'm not sure I'm up to it.'

She looked into his eye. 'I understand. But that's not my feeling. I think you're a very capable man who needs to find his way back from a terribly dark place.'

'You're a trick-cyclist as well?'

She shook her head slightly. 'No, not a psychiatrist. Just an extremely good judge of character.'

He finished his tea and sat back in the chair. 'I don't know . . . sorry.'

'Hey, don't be sorry. I really do understand. Look, I'm going home for my brother's birthday tomorrow. Why don't you come with me? You might enjoy it. And we can get to know each other.'

'Oh, I'm not sure I'm ready for civilised company, love.'

She laughed. 'Think about it. I'll message you later. I'll be leaving for Scotland about ten o'clock. It'll be an overnighter.'

'Scotland?'

'Yes. We, the family that is, have a place just south of Edinburgh.'

'Ah, okay.'

She took out her purse.

He put his hand on her arm. 'Hey, it's okay. I can still spring for a couple of coffees.'

She looked at the scars again. 'Of course.'

'Do you want my number?'

As she stood up, she said. 'I found you, didn't I?' She winked. 'I have your number.'

Chapter Three
'Mr Brown'

As Shackleton walked back to his office, he considered what Amanda Lang had said. He looked at his watch. It was just after ten. The wind off the water had turned chilly and a few rain clouds were building over the Pennine Hills. His phone beeped. He didn't recognise the number. He swiped the screen, then smiled. *Thanks for coffee. Amanda x.*

Back in his office he removed the eyepatch, then checked the laptop for emails. One from a guy who wanted him to check on his wife. Another from a small company wanting background information on some staff. 'Not exactly Sam Spade, stuff,' he said aloud. He replied to both mails then went to the window. He watched the raindrops run down the glass, then raised his arm and sniffed. 'Jesus, I stink.'

The rear of the office had a couple of rooms that served as his flat. He stripped off and stood in front of the bathroom mirror. The four days of stubble needed to go. After shaving, he showered and put on clean jeans and a sweater. He'd arranged a meeting with the guy, about his wife, at one o'clock in town. He grabbed his raincoat, slipped the eyepatch back on and headed out to the tram. Twenty-five minutes later, he was in his regular bar on Deansgate.

'Morning, mate. The usual?' said the barman.

Shack dropped a ten pound note on the counter. 'Yeah, please. How are you doing?'

'Same shit, different day.' The barman put a pint of Stella and a small single malt in front of him.

Shack picked up the whisky and downed it in one. 'Ain't that the truth.'

At five minutes to one, and two more pints later, his prospective client walked in. The man had been instructed to go to the end of the bar, next to the serving hatch, and wait.

Shack swallowed the last of his beer, then watched the man for a minute or two. He wore a Peaky Blinders cap low over his forehead and dark glasses. The overcoat was expensive, the collar up. Shack walked over and held out his hand. '*Mr Brown*?'

'Yes.'

'Shackleton Blister.' As they shook hands, Shack noticed the big Omega. 'Would you like a drink?'

'No, nothing, thank you.'

'Okay. Let's get a booth over here.' When they sat down, Shack said, 'You'd look less conspicuous if you took off the hat and shades, *Mr Brown*.'

The man smiled at Shack's emphasis on the name *Brown*. 'I guess you know that's not my real name, Mr Blister.'

'Call me Shack . . . I don't follow United, but I do know who you are.'

'You're a Manchester City fan then?'

'No, I just don't follow soccer that much, sorry.'

Brown gave a little smile. 'No problem.'

'So, what can I do for you, Mr B?'

The man looked around the bar, no one seemed to be paying them any attention. He took an envelope from his pocket. 'There is a photograph of my wife in here.'

Shack leaned forward and said quietly. 'I know who she is.'

Again, *Brown* gave a slight smile. 'Yes of course. My cellphone number is in there, along with a photo of her cars and our address in Wilmslow. She uses the Bentley the most.'

'And why not?' said Shack. 'Okay, what is it you want me to do?'

This time *Brown* leaned forward. 'I think she's been seeing one of my teammates.'

'Why do you think that?'

'She comes to the games. She never did. She comes to the away fixtures as well, which she hated.'

'Maybe she's just fallen in love with the beautiful game?'

Brown shook his head. 'I doubt that. Look can you help me?'

'Yeah, sure. If it's what you want. My fee is five-hundred a day, plus expenses. Minimum two days, upfront. I'll bill you after that, and I'll need to be paid in cash, please.'

Brown nodded. 'I'll give you a grand a day, including expenses. I don't need any invoice and I don't want any paper trail.'

Shack offered his hand. As they shook, he said, 'Okay. When do you want me to start?'

'How about tomorrow?'

'No, sorry. I think I might be going away for the weekend. I'll be back in Manchester on Sunday sometime. So how about Monday?'

'Okay, fine. You want the two-grand now?'

Shack raised his eyebrows. 'You carry that much cash?'

Brown looked around the bar again, then turned sideways. He put his hat on the seat next to him. Shack watched as he went into the inside pocket of his coat. The cap was then placed on the table with two one-thousand pound bundles underneath.

Shack quickly transferred the money to his raincoat pocket. 'Right. I'll be in touch, *Mr Brown.*'

Chapter Four
'Ruby'

The meeting with the footballer had not taken long and would be reasonably lucrative in the short term. As Shack walked along Deansgate he took out his phone and tapped a number. It was several rings before the call was answered.

'Hello, Shack.' A woman's voice.

'Ruby, hi. How are you doing, gorgeous?'

'Always busy. You?'

'Not as much as you I'd guess.' He heard her little laugh. 'Can you fit me in today?'

'Twice in a week. Sure, baby. It's always lovely to see you.'

'When are you free?'

'Anytime between five and nine.

'Great. See you about six then.'

After speaking to Ruby, he stepped into a doorway and called for an Uber. It wasn't long until the taxi pulled-up at the kerbside. Twenty minutes later the cab stopped in front of a large office building. Shack tipped the driver a couple of quid, then stepped out. In the foyer, he waited for the lift with a couple of other people. One of the men looked away, after Shack noticed him staring at the eyepatch. He got out on the fifth floor and went to the Reception Desk. The guy behind the counter recognised him. 'Good afternoon, sir.'

Shack smiled. 'Hello again. I'm meeting Stella Davidson. I'm a little early.'

'It's okay, she's free. Go right down, sir.'

'Thanks.'

The notice on the door said. *Stella Davidson. Human Assets*. Shack smiled at the wording and knocked.

'Come in.'

'Afternoon, Stella.'

The woman stood and smiled. 'Hi, Shack. How have you been?'

'I'm okay, thanks.'

'Have a seat. You want some tea?'

He shook his head. 'I'm fine. So, you have some new people?'

'Yes, we're expanding. We have three candidates we need to run due diligence on.'

Shack supressed a smile at the terminology. 'Okay. Usual rates?'

Davidson nodded. 'Usual rates. Usual Confidentiality.'

'When do you need it?'

'No later than month end. Can you do that?'

'Two weeks. Yeah, no problem. Maybe sooner.'

She slid a folder across the desk. 'Details.'

'Okay, cheers. I'll be in touch, Stella.' Once outside he checked the time again, just after three. Another Uber and he was back across the city. The cab stopped outside *The Cavalier* pub, a block away from Ruby's place. The bar was busy with businessmen and shoppers alike. He ordered a sandwich, a pint and a small malt, then took a seat near the entrance.

It was a few minutes to six, when he pressed the intercom at Ruby's apartment building.

'Come up, Shack.'

He smiled at the sound of her voice. There was a buzz and the door clicked open. When he got to her flat, she was standing in the doorway. She smiled, reached up and kissed him. 'Twice in one week. Lucky me.'

Two hours later he placed three hundred pounds on the table. She stood close to him and frowned. 'I've told you, you don't need to do that, Shack.'

'I know, Ruby, but a girl's gotta make a living.'

She put her arms around his neck. 'Yeah, I guess,' she kissed him. 'I still have another hour, baby.'

'I'd love to stay, but I got a couple of things to do.' As he dressed, he said, 'How did that lead go with the flat?'

She smiled. 'Yeah, I bought it. Thanks for the heads up on that. It was a great price.'

'How many is that now?'

'Five, including this one.'

'Nice. You're building quite a little portfolio, Ruby.' He nodded towards the bed. 'So why're you still doing this?'

'I like this, and as you know, I only have a select clientele now. So, it's no hardship.' She winked. 'But I'd quit in a heartbeat, if the right guy asked me to.' She picked up his eyepatch and handed it to him. 'Wanna ask me to, Shack?'

He slipped on the patch, then touched her cheek. 'You can do better than me, gorgeous.'

'Oh, I don't think so.'

'I'm almost forty and live in the back of a rented office.' He raised his hands. 'And then there are these.'

She took a hand in hers and ran her fingers gently over the scars. 'This isn't ugly. This is a badge of courage.' She touched the scars on his neck. 'You tried to save your wife from a burning car. These are nothing to be ashamed of.'

He kissed her hand, then pointed to the eyepatch. 'And this?'

She frowned. 'Yes, well, that's another thing, isn't it? They don't make it easy for a cop in prison. And to be honest, baby, the loss of an eye was not that bad. You were lucky that's all you lost.'

He raised an eyebrow. 'Ain't that the truth.'

'So? Are you gonna ask me?'

'What?'

'To quit.'

He smiled. 'Oh, Ruby. I'm not for you.'

She touched his cheek. 'You're a good man, Shack. You're gentle and kind and funny. That's all a woman really wants.'

He took her face in his hands and kissed her. 'See you soon, love. Take care, eh?'

The tram back to his building in Salford Quays was quiet. He took out his phone and swiped the screen. He looked at the number for several seconds, then tapped out a text. A couple of minutes later the phone pinged an incoming. He touched the screen and smiled as he read the message. *Great. It'll be black-tie but wear what you like. Pick you up at 10. Amanda x.*

Chapter Five
'Eau de Glenfiddich'

He'd spent the previous evening going through the background details Stella Davidson had given him. An hour on the laptop had added further information to the bundle. A few days of foot-work, when he got back from Scotland, would be enough to give Stella what she needed and a nice five grand in his bank account. *Mr Brown's* case would need a bit of running around, but nothing too difficult.

This morning he'd packed an over-night bag and a suit-carrier. He'd downed a bacon sandwich, a pot of tea and three Paracetamol. Now he awaited the arrival of Amanda Lang. At two minutes to ten his phone pinged. He swiped the screen. *I'm outside.*

As he left the building, the tailgate of a Range Rover Evoque flipped slowly open. He dropped in his luggage, then stepped back as the hatch closed.

'Morning,' he said as he got into the passenger seat.

She smiled. 'Good morning. How are you today?'

He clipped on the seat belt and nodded. 'Yeah, I'm good.'

As she pulled away from the kerb, she said, 'You smell nice. What is that?'

He looked at her for a second, then said, 'Hugo Boss.'

'Hmm, I like it. Far better than, Eau de Glenfiddich!'

He looked at her again, one eyebrow raised. Then grinned.

The drive north was pleasant. The weather was good and, once they'd cleared Manchester, the traffic steady on the M6 and A74. They made small talk, but nothing about their respective partner's deaths. Amanda did try to touch on the crash, but it was clear he was not ready to re-live it with her, for now anyway.

At Abington, they turned off the motorway and headed north east towards the Pentland Hills. Three and a half hours after leaving Manchester, they drove through the little village of Penicuick. A few minutes later they turned off the road and passed through two large open gates. The elegant sign at the side of the entrance read, *LONGDRAY MANOR.*

A half mile down the treelined drive the car pulled up to the front of the impressive 15th century pile. Longdray had always been referred to as *The Manor* but, in real terms, it was a fair-sized castle set in four hundred acres of beautiful West Lothian countryside.

'Nice hotel,' said Shack. He frowned. 'Not sure I can afford this though, love.'

She reached over the seat and grabbed her handbag. 'Oh, don't worry. I can get us a pretty good rate here.'

Shack climbed out as the tailgate flipped open. He went to collect their bags, then heard a voice behind. 'Good afternoon, sir. I'll take care of your luggage.'

He turned and nodded, 'Ah, okay. Thanks.'

As she came around the car, the man smiled. 'Good afternoon, Lady Amanda. Welcome home, madam.'

She touched the old retainer's arm. 'Hello, Connor. Lovely to be back.'

'Lady Amanda? Welcome home?' said Shack.

She smiled at the puzzled look on his face. 'This isn't a hotel, Shack. It's my family's home.' She linked her arm through his and, as they entered the huge hallway, said, 'Welcome to *Longdray Manor.*'

Chapter Six
'A Nice Laphroaig'

Longdray Manor had been the family seat of the Lang family for over six hundred years. Gifted by King James the 5th of Scotland, to the first Earl of Longdray, for services rendered. It was rumoured the *services rendered* were decidedly dubious in nature, including anything from procuring ladies of the court, to spying and even bumping off the odd threat to the throne.

Lord Geoffrey Gonville Lang, the 9th Earl of Longdray and current incumbent, was Amanda Lang's father.

As Shack and Amanda entered the huge drawing room, Lord Lang stood up. With a happy smile and arms wide, he welcomed his daughter. 'Amanda, my darling.'

Their embrace lasted several seconds, followed by kissed cheeks. 'How are you, Daddy? It's lovely to see you.'

'Oh, I'm fine, despite what the damn quacks say. And who is this young fella?'

She linked her arm through his. 'Daddy, this is my friend, Shackleton Blister. Shack, this is my father, Geoffrey.'

The old man stepped forward; hand outstretched. 'A pleasure to meet you, my boy. Shackleton, marvellous name, marvellous name.'

As they shook hands, Shack said, 'Pleasure's all mine, sir. As is the surprise.' He looked past the man for a second and raised an eyebrow at Amanda.

'Surprise? What surprise?'

She frowned. 'Oh, that's my fault, Daddy. I didn't tell Shack exactly where we were going. And when we arrived at *Longdray* it was a bit of a surprise.'

'Ah, I see. Yes, it is rather a lump of a place, isn't it?'

It's magnificent, sir. And I'm delighted to be here.'

'Call me Geoffrey. And you are most welcome.'

'So, where is the birthday boy?' said Amanda.

'He's in Edinburgh. Be back this afternoon.'

The door burst open and a woman in riding habit rushed in. 'Amanda!' She dashed over and they hugged. 'It's great you could come.' She turned and looked at Shack. 'And you've brought a friend.'

'Abigail, this is, Shackleton.   Shack, my sister, Abigail.'

The younger sister beamed, then shook hands. 'Hello, there.'

'How about some tea?' said Geoffrey. He winked at Shack. 'Or maybe something stronger?'

'Daddy, it's not even two o'clock,' chided Amanda. 'I'll get some tea.'

Lord Lang raised a hand, 'Shackleton, over here, my boy.'

Shack joined him at a small table in front of the big windows. A couple of crystal decanters and a few glasses sparkled in the afternoon sun. The old man picked up a decanter. 'We've a very nice Laphroaig here. What do you say?'

Shack smiled. 'I say, I'll have a large one, please.'

The old Lord laughed out loud. 'Excellent, excellent.'

On the other side of the drawing room, Amanda shook her head. Abigail moved closer and said quietly, 'Where

31

on earth did you find such a brooding piratical Heathcliff? He's positively edible.'

Amanda shook her head again. 'Abby, you are such a tart sometimes.'

Chapter Seven
'Chrissy'

That evening Shack slipped on the eyepatch, then went to the long mirror. It had been a while since he wore his evening suit. He'd lost weight, but the suit still looked okay.

In the mirror, Chrissy stood behind him. She smiled. 'You look so handsome, Bobby.'

He smiled back at her. A tear rolled down his cheek.

She stepped closer; her voice soft, gentle. 'It's okay, darling. It's okay. I love you.'

The knock on the bedroom door made him turn. The room was empty. 'Come in,' he shouted.

'Are you decent?'

'That's debatable,' he said, as he brushed the tear from his face.

'Goodness me, Mr Blister. You do scrub-up well.'

He laughed. 'Yeah. Been a while since I had a chance to wear this.'

'And you certainly wear it well.'

'Thanks. So, what's the plan?'

'Downstairs now, for drinks with the family, then an early dinner at half past six. Guests will start to arrive around eight o'clock. Then it's all out to the marquee.'

'Okay. Sounds good.'

'Are you hungry?'

'Not really, but I'll eat. Could murder a beer though.'

'I'm sure we can find you one.' She flicked a tiny piece of something from his shoulder. then linked her arm though his. 'Shall we?'

He grinned. Yes, M'lady.'

As he closed the door he glanced back at the mirror. Only his reflection looked back.

Chapter Eight
'Good Morning'

The birthday celebrations had gone on until daylight, but Shackleton had left well before then. Amanda's brother played rugby at the local amateur club and several of his bekilted teammates were in attendance. By midnight Shack, and most of the hundred or so guests, had seen more bare backsides than a proctologist surgery on a busy Monday. So, after saying goodnight to Amanda, he was in bed by one o'clock. Thankfully his room was at the front of the property, so little could be heard from the revellers in the marquee on the rear lawn. He hadn't drunk as much as usual, but enough to help him sleep.

It was a little after eight when the sound of vehicles in the drive woke him. He went to the window and saw several caterer's vans moving around to the rear. He pulled open the big sash window and sucked in the fresh morning air. There was a light drizzle, and the breeze sprinkled a few tiny drops on his face. He closed his good eye and leaned out, enjoying the simple pleasure of the raindrops.

'Good morning.'

Below the window Abigail Lang sat astride a magnificent horse.

He waved. 'Morning.'

'Just off for a ride. Care to join me?'

'Not my thing. Sorry, Abby.'

'Shame. Okay, see you later.' She tapped the animal's rump with her whip and trotted off.

His phone beeped. He picked it up and looked at the screen, *Amanda Calling.* 'Morning?'

'Good morning, Shack. You're up and about then.'

'Yeah. Whatsup?'

'Just to see if you want any breakfast. It's laid out in the dining room. I'll be down there at nine.'

'Not sure I want anything to eat. but I'll be down for some tea.'

'Okay, see you soon.'

Several of the more genteel houseguests were milling around at the bottom of the staircase, when Shack came down. He nodded and said, 'Good morning,' to a couple he'd met the night before, then went into the dining room. More houseguests were seated around the big table, a few helped themselves to food from a huge sideboard service.

Connor saw him and came over. 'Good morning, sir. Are you taking breakfast?'

'No thanks. Just some tea please.'

'Tea for me as well please, Connor,' said Amanda.

Shack turned around. 'Morning . . . again.'

She smiled. 'How did you sleep?'

'Fine, no problem, thanks.'

'Did you enjoy the party?'

'Yeah, it was okay.'

'Not your cup of tea, eh?'

'It was okay. What's not to like about free booze. So, what's the plan for getting back?'

'I want to spend a little time with my father before we go. But we could get away by midday. If that's alright?'

'Sounds good.'

'Your tea, madam, sir.'

36

'Thank you, Connor. Has my father come down yet?'

'Yes, madam. His Lordship is in the study.'

'Okay, thank you.' She turned to Shack. 'I think I'll take my tea in there. You'll be alright here?'

He nodded. 'I'm fine. Might have a bit of fresh air after this.'

'Good idea. But it's starting to get heavy out there. There're are coats and umbrellas in the boot room. Left hand side of the hall.'

'Right, thanks.'

She touched his arm and smiled. 'See you later.'

Chapter Nine
'Oh, Your Ladyship'

It was almost twelve-thirty, when Amanda and Shack left *Longdray Manor*. The weather had brightened, and the sun peeked through what was left of the rainclouds. As they drove through the big gates, Amanda said, 'Are you okay?'

He glanced at her. 'Yeah, sure. Why?'

'You seem a little pre-occupied this morning.'

'Sorry, just thinking about some stuff I need to do when we get back.'

'Right, so we haven't ruined a weekend for you.'

'It was fine. A change to be with some nice people.'

By the time they'd slipped onto the A74, they'd pretty much exhausted the small talk, much of which revolved around the previous night's celebrations.

She took a deep breath. 'You never once asked about my mother?'

Without looking at her, he said, 'I guessed you'd tell me about her if you wanted to.'

There was silence for several seconds. 'She died from breast cancer almost ten years ago.'

'I'm sorry. Were you close? Sorry that's stupid, of course you'd be.'

'Yes, we were. She was a wonderful mother. She never met Samantha, but I'm sure she would have loved her. And Abby still struggles with the loss. We all miss her very much. My father more than anyone.'

He sighed. 'I can understand that.'

'Oh, Shack I'm sorry. I didn't mean to cause any sadness.'

'You didn't . . . It's always there, love.'

'You want to talk about the accident?'

He shook his head.

They drove in silence for several miles, then she said, 'So, Mr B, are we going to work together?'

'You really think we can do anything? You really think we can get justice?'

'I do. I have a lot of information that Sam left. And if we pool our resources, we could be a formidable team.'

He chuckled. 'Sorry to disappoint you, love, but I don't have any resources.'

She flashed him a quick look, then turned her attention back to the road. 'You have a brain, don't you?'

Again, he chuckled. 'Debatable.'

'So, you're happy to do nothing? You just let these bastards continue to do whatever they want with impunity?'

He looked at her and smiled. 'Oh, Y'Ladyship! Such language.'

She laughed. 'Yes, well, I can swear if the situation calls for it.'

'Okay, well that makes all the difference. I'd be more than happy to work with a foul-mouthed aristocrat.'

They both laughed.

It was late afternoon when the Range Rover pulled up in front of Shack's building. Before getting out he said, 'Thanks for the weekend. It was good.'

She frowned. 'Well, I suppose I'll believe you.'

He grinned. 'It was okay. Really, thanks.'

'So, when can you come down to London?'

'I've two small cases I need to work on before I leave. Shouldn't take more than a week.'

'Oh, right.'

He climbed out and collected his bags from the rear. She came round the car. 'Listen, why don't I stay on here in Manchester, and help you?'

He frowned. 'What?'

'With your cases. Maybe I can help, and you get finished quicker?'

'I don't think so, love. Can't have a journalist involved. I'd lose what's left of my reputation. For whatever that's worth.'

'I can be discreet if need be.' She winked.

Shack stepped back as the tailgate slowly closed. He looked at her. *She was good company,* he thought. 'Okay. But you can't use anything.'

She held up her hand. 'I promise. Guides honour.'

'Really? You were in the Girl Guides?'

'Well no, but . . .'

He smiled. 'Okay, okay. Where are you staying?'

'I'm at the *Hilton*.'

'Right, I'll message you later.'

She leaned forward and kissed his cheek. 'See you soon, partner.'

Chapter Ten
'What's The Caper'

The next morning, Shack pulled up to the front of the *Hilton* a few minutes after ten o'clock. Deansgate, as usual, was busy and a black-cab came to a sudden stop behind Shack's car, the driver beeping his horn for him to get out of the way. Shack stuck his hand out of the window and waved the irate cabbie around, just as Amanda climbed in. 'Good morning. Upsetting the locals already, Mr B?'

'Morning. Yeah, well I got to get my fun from somewhere.' She smelled good. And in jeans and a short leather jacket, looked appropriately casual. 'How're you doing?' he said.

'I'm fine thanks. Looking forward to this. So, what's the caper, partner?'

He turned to her and raised an eyebrow. 'Caper?'

In an over-affected American accent, she continued. 'Yeah . . . caper. Ain't that what you Private Dicks call it?'

He laughed. 'Right, yeah. But to be honest, I'm not a Private Detective. I'd need a licence for that and being an ex-con . . . well you understand.'

'Ah, okay. So, what do you call yourself?'

He glanced at her for a second. 'I undertake confidential enquires.'

'What's the difference?'

He winked. 'Semantics.'

She smiled. 'Well, as far as I'm concerned, you're a genuine Private Dick.'

He laughed again. 'Cheshire.'

'What?'

'You asked what the caper was. We're off to Cheshire. Wilmslow to be exact.'

'Okay. To do what?'

'Follow a lady. See what she gets up to.'

'Sounds a little boring.'

'Most of it is, love.'

The house in Wilmslow was opulent, with high perimeter walls and sturdy gates at the entrance. Several CCTV cameras were visible. Shack parked the car to offer a view of the front of the property. Through the gates he could clearly see a Bentley Continental and a 4x4 Jaguar. He looked at his watch. He'd received a message from *Mr Brown* earlier. *She will be leaving around eleven to meet girlfriends.*

Shack leaned over the seat and picked up a bottle of Coke and a bottle of water. He handed her the water. 'Here you go.'

She shook her head. 'No, I'm fine for now. Thank you. So, what do we do?'

He cracked the Coke and swallowed half the contents. 'When she comes out, we follow her.'

'That's it?'

'Yep. That's it.' He grinned. 'All pretty exciting stuff, eh?'

'And if you wait here, and she doesn't come out?'

'I'll make a judgement call if that happens.'

She frowned, 'And what if we need the bathroom?'

He finished off the Coke and waved the empty bottle. 'We have these.' He laughed at the shocked look on her face. 'I'm kidding, Y'Ladyship.'

She punched his arm, then laughed as well, just as the big gates slowly opened.

Chapter Eleven
'Three Days Later'

By Thursday afternoon Shack was happy he'd got enough information on *Mr Brown's* wife. They'd followed her all day, every day, since Monday. They had gone to the United and Chelsea home game at Old Trafford and watched her every move. Amanda had proved useful as she was able to get into a couple of places Shack could not, like the lady's powder room in *The Ivy,* and the dressing rooms in *Harvey Nichols.*

In his office, Shack printed off the photos and the six page report for *Mr Brown.* A meeting had been set, in the Deansgate bar, for six that evening.

The background checks for Stella Davidson's new staff were ninety-five percent complete and a couple of hours writing-up his findings would be done the next morning.

He looked at his watch. Almost three-thirty. He picked up the phone and called Amanda.

It was several rings before a sleepy voice answered. 'Hello, Shack.'

'Hi. Sorry, did I wake you?'

'Yes . . . It's okay. I dozed off. Sorry. What's up, partner?'

He smiled. 'Okay. I've finished the *Brown* report and I'm meeting him at six in town. I thought we could go together and eat somewhere nice afterwards?'

'That sounds good. And you said you were pretty much done with the other work?'

'Yeah. I just need to write it up in the morning and get that off to Stella. So, if you've had enough of Manchester, we could head down to London tomorrow?'

'Okay, great. So, where are we meeting the footballer?'

'A bar on Deansgate. *The Merchants*. You can walk to it from the Hilton, it's only three blocks up. I'll be there at five-thirty.'

'Right, I'll see you then.'

He looked at the phone for several seconds then swiped the screen and tapped another name.

'Shack. Hi, baby.'

'Hello, gorgeous. How're you doing?'

'Think I'm getting a cold, but I'm okay.'

'Listen, Ruby . . . I'm going down to London for a while.'

'Okay. When are you back?'

'Not sure, but if you need anything, call me.'

'You're very protective all of a sudden. Is everything okay?'

'Yeah, yeah, no problems. I'm just not sure what my plans are gonna be, once I get down there.'

'Should I be worried, baby?'

'No. It's fine. I just wanted to let you know.'

'You got time to see me before you leave?'

'As tempting as that is, I've a few things to do. I'll stay in touch.'

'Okay. Take care, Shack. I'll miss you.'

He smiled at the sound of her kisses. 'You too, gorgeous.'

It was almost twenty-to-six when Amanda entered *The Merchants*. Shack had been there since five and was on his second pint of Stella.

She saw him at the far end of the room and joined him in the booth. 'It's quite nice in here.'

He frowned. 'You were expecting something a little seedier?'

'No, sorry, I didn't mean . . .'

'I'm kidding. Do you want a drink?'

'Pino would be nice.'

He stood and went to the bar. A few minutes later he returned with her wine and another beer for himself. He chinked her glass. 'Cheers.'

'So, our guy is here at six?'

'Yeah. But you'll need to make yourself scarce when he arrives.'

'Aww.'

'Sorry, love. I can't . . .'

This time she grinned. 'I'm kidding!'

At five-to-six, Shack said, 'He's here.'

Amanda picked up her glass and went over to the bar. The footballer, again, wore an expensive overcoat, cap and shades. As he sat down opposite Shack, he removed the hat and glasses.

'*Mr Brown*, good evening. Drink?'

Brown shook his head. 'Evening. So, what do you have?'

Shack slid a large brown envelope across the table. 'It's all in here.'

Brown made to open the envelope. Shack put his hand on it. 'You want to do that here?'

'Hmm, yeah. Suppose not. What do I owe you?'

'Three and a half days, so another fifteen hundred, please.'

The money was passed across under the hat. 'Thanks. If I can help in the future, you know how to find me.'

Brown put on his glasses and hat. 'No offence, but I hope not.'

'None taken. Good luck.' He lowered his voice. 'You had a cracking game on Wednesday night by the way.'

The footballer nodded. 'Thanks. Bye.'

The *San Carlo* was busy, but the receptionist said they could have a table if they vacated by eight o'clock.

'This is nice,' said Amanda.

'And quite apt considering I'll be using the soccer player's dosh to pay for it.'

'What do you mean?'

He leaned forward. 'This place is regularly frequented by footballers and celebs alike.'

'Ah, I see. Well you can save his money. Dinner is on me.'

'Really? Okay, if you insist, Y'Ladyship.'

'I do.'

He grinned. 'In that case, I'm gonna have Tournedos Rossini.'

Food ordered and wine served, Amanda asked, 'What did *Mr Brown* say?'

'About what?'

She sighed. 'About his wife.'

'Never said anything. I just gave him the report.'

'That's a shame. It would have been nice to see his face, when he found out his wife wasn't having an affair.'

'Yeah. But I wonder what he's going to think when he finds out she's . . .'

The waiter interrupted. 'Excuse me, madam, sir. Tournedos Rossini and a Sea Bass?'

Chapter Twelve
'Bon Appetite'

Friday morning was warm. By ten o'clock the temperature was already in the twenties and set to get hotter. Amanda had checked out of the *Hilton*, then picked Shack up from his place. By midday they were on the motorway to London. The M6 was kind to them and the usual pain-in-the-arse drive south, was not unpleasant. It was a little after 4pm when they pulled into the underground parking of Amanda's building in Hammersmith. They unloaded the luggage and took the lift to the ground floor. In the reception area, she said, 'I'll just let them know I'm back.'

He nodded and watched as she chatted away to the concierge. A few moments later she returned with several envelopes and a couple of packages. He hit the lift call-button, then once inside said, 'Floor?'

'Seven. Top floor.'

He smiled. 'Hmm, of course. Didn't think you'd be on any other.'

She dug him in the ribs with her elbow.

'Ouch!'

The lift pinged and the doors slid quietly open. At her flat, she juggled with her luggage as she tapped in the access code. Once inside, she dropped everything on the floor. 'Oh, God, it's good to be home.'

Shack whistled at the vista through the huge patio windows. 'Wow. Now that's a view.'

He went to the window and looked out across the Thames and down to Hammersmith bridge, a hundred yards to the left. 'This is very nice, Y'Ladyship.'

'Thank you. Yes we were lucky to get it. A friend of ours was selling-up and moving to Dubai. Needed a quick sale, so we got quite a bargain . . . Tea?'

'Rather have a beer, if you have one, please?'

'Okay, I think I'll have one too. Your room is this way. Let's dump the luggage then have a drink on the balcony.'

After their beers, Amanda said, 'Okay, what about dinner? I have nothing in so we can order a takeaway, or go out?'

'I'm happy with a pizza and another of these,' he held up the bottle, 'if that's all right?'

'Sure. There are several good Italians around here. Order me a special from Giovani's, please. The menu's in the drawer under the phone. I'm going to shower and change.'

He smiled. 'Yes, ma'am.'

By the time Amanda had returned, the food had been delivered. She came out on to the balcony to find the table laid with a cloth, the pizzas on plates, a large bowl of salad and a bottle of Pino Grigio in a cooler. She smiled. 'Oh, this is nice. Thank you.'

He poured her wine, then chinked his beer-bottle against her glass. 'Bon appetite, Y'Ladyship.'

After dinner, she brought out a ten year old Macallan. 'Would you like something a little stronger to finish off with?'

'Don't mind if I do.'

She put the bottle and a crystal tumbler in front of him. 'Help yourself.'

He poured a generous tot, then swirled the amber liquid. He sniffed the heady aroma. 'Mmm, that's nice.'

'Okay, Mr Shackleton Blister. To business.'

He swallowed the whisky and poured another. 'I'm all ears. What's your plan?'

'We really need to go through all Samantha's evidence, then we make a plan.'

'Good. You up to looking at it now?'

'We can't until Monday.'

Shack frowned. 'Why?'

'Because it's in a safe-deposit, at the bank.'

He smiled. 'Right, then let's use tonight to do a bit of investigating ourselves.'

'What do you have in mind?'

'The nightclub. Where she was killed.' He looked at her face. 'You okay to go there?'

She took a deep breath. He saw the tears well-up.

'It's okay, love. I can go myself.'

She wiped her eyes. 'No. No, I'm fine. We'll go tonight.'

He gently touched her hand, then winked. 'So, we're going clubbing.'

Chapter Thirteen
'Bobby's Gone'

Idols is one of Soho's swishest nightclubs. The once grand old cinema, is now a multi-level fun palace dedicated to satisfying the hedonistic desires of its varied clientele. Celebrities, politicians, and villains, rub shoulders with lesser mortals, but only those whose bank balance can withstand the exorbitantly outrageous prices.

It was a little before eleven, when the Uber came to a stop at the end of Frith Street. 'Can't get any further up here guys, sorry. Hope this is okay?' said the driver.

Amanda handed him a couple of pounds tip. 'Thank you. It's fine.'

The street was packed with Friday night-revellers, drinking, shouting and laughing. The music belted out from the cafés and bars, which lined the street, fuelling the party atmosphere and welcoming another London weekend.

'Have you been to this club before, Shack?' said Amanda, as they eased their way through the party people.

He guided a drunk out of their way. 'Yeah. I know the place. I haven't been here since before the . . . well, a while.'

She linked her arm though his and they carried on through the ever growing throng. 'Maybe we should have left it for a quieter night?'

'Nah, busier the better, love. Gives us a little cover.'

'Right. Hide in plain sight?'

'In theory, yeah. Okay, we're down here.' He removed the eyepatch and slipped it in his pocket. Then took a pair of tinted glasses from his jacket and put them on.

'Very trendy, Mr B. And not as noticeable as the patch, eh?'

He squeezed her arm. 'Correct.'

There was a queue of about seventy people waiting at the door to *Idols*. Another shorter queue was obviously for people on the VIP list. Three very fit-looking men guarded the entrance to the pleasure palace.

Amanda made to join the long line, but Shack eased her forward. 'Come on.' At the door he slapped one of the gatekeepers on the back. 'Hey, Donny!'

The man turned, clearly not recognising Shack. Then the stern face turned to a smile. 'Bloody hell. Bobby Stone. Jesus, man, I thought you were dead.'

Amanda watched as the two men hugged.

'How've you been, Donny? Surprised to see you still working the doors.'

'I own Sentinel Security now. Bought it a couple of months ago. But I still like to do the odd night on the cobbles.'

'Cool. Congratulations, mate. So, any chance we can buy you a drink once we get in?'

Donny looked at the clipboard, then said sternly, 'You're not on the sheet, Bobby?'

'No, we . . .'

'I'm kidding, for fuck 'sake,' he quickly unclipped the thick blue barrier rope. 'See you at the bar later.'

Shack nodded. 'Look forward to it. Cheers, mate.'

As they walked up the steps, Amanda said, 'I really like the name Bobby.'

He stopped and glared at her. 'My name's Shackleton. Bobby's gone. Okay?'

She backed away from him. 'I'm sorry, I...'

He saw the shock on her face, then touched her arm. 'No, no. I'm sorry. I didn't mean to snap at you. I just...'

She linked her arm back through his and smiled. 'Hey, it's fine, Really.'

He squeezed her arm against his side. *I like this woman,* he thought.

Donny watched as Shack and Amanda went inside, then took out his phone and quickly tapped in a message. *Bobby Stone has just showed up at Idols!!!!!*

Chapter Fourteen
'What A Sleaze'

The club was filling up, the VIP area already crowded. Shack recognised a couple of celebs, a minor royal and a politician, as well as at least one local villain. At the bar Amanda ordered two beers from a Marilyn Monroe look-alike. Handing one to Shack, she said, 'This is some place.'

He leaned forward and shouted over the music, 'What?'

She raised her voice. 'I said, this is some place.'

He took the bottle and tapped it against her's. 'Cheers. Yeah, not the sort of gaff your used to, eh, Y'Ladyship?'

'Oh, I don't know, I can be quite Bacchanalian occasionally.'

He grinned. 'Yeah, right.'

They sipped from the bottles then Shack said. 'Over here. Away from the bloody speaker.'

They moved to a raised area on the other side of the room and found a tall table to stand against. 'Better?' he said.

'A bit. So, what's the plan, partner?'

'Let's just see who's about first. Then I want to have a look out back.'

'Out back?'

He looked at her and moved closer. 'Yeah, if you're okay with it, we should check out where Samantha was found.'

She took another sip of beer and nodded. 'Sure.'

A few minutes later a youngish, Brad Pitt look-alike, said. 'Any more drinks, guys?'

Shack nodded and held up his bottle. 'Two more, please.'

Brad smiled and headed for the bar.

They were halfway through the second beer when Donny arrived. 'So, how've you been, Bobby?' he grinned, 'and where the hell've you been?'

'Went back up north a couple of years ago. Just down in the Smoke for the weekend.'

'Right. Heard you'd been in a bad accident?'

'Yeah? Who told you that?'

'Err, not sure, mate. Just word on the cobbles. Heard you left the police as well?'

'You hear that on the cobbles too, Donny?'

The bouncer frowned. 'Hey, chill mate. I'm just talking here.'

'Yeah, sorry . . . Bit of a problem a while ago, so moved back home.'

Donny smiled. 'Cool. Manchester's cool. And who's this lovely lady?'

'This is Caroline. Caroline, this is Donny Black, an old pal from way back.'

The big man took her hand and kissed it. 'My pleasure.'

Amanda controlled the cringe and smiled. 'Hi.'

'Can I get you a drink, mate?'

'Maybe later, when I've finished on the door.' He winked and nodded towards Amanda. 'That's if you haven't split by then.' He put his hand to his ear-piece, then said into the head-mic. 'I'll be right there.' He turned back to Shack. 'Okay, mate. Duty calls. Catch you later.'

Shack nodded. Then he and Amanda watched as the bouncer cut a swathe through the crowd. 'What a sleaze,' she said.

Shack swallowed the last of his beer. 'Okay, Caroline, let's check-out the back.'

She put her bottle on the table. 'Caroline?'

'Yeah. No need to give out any more info than need be,' he winked, 'Caroline.'

Chapter Fifteen
'Chalky'

The rear of the club backed onto a small service road. Several recycling skips, steel beer kegs and bundles of cardboard, were stored neatly along the wall. A couple of streetlights provided some illumination. A homeless person approached. 'Spare some change please, sir?'

Shack took a couple of pound coins from his pocket and handed it to the bedraggled man. 'You stay around here, mate?'

'What?'

'You stay around here? You in this street regular?'

'Why? Who wants to know?'

Shack took out his wallet and fished out a fiver. 'I want to know. Do you stay around here? It's not a problem. You're not in any bother.'

The man made to take the note. Shack pulled it away. 'Well?'

'There's a doorway.' He pointed to the other end of the street. 'With a vent that's pretty warm. I use that most nights.'

Shack gave him the fiver then took out another. 'A woman was killed in this street about three months ago. You here then?'

The man made to walk away. 'I had fuck all to do with that.'

'Hold on. It's okay.' Shack took out a tenner and waved the two notes in front of the guy. 'We just need to know if you saw anything. It was a friend of mine who died. We're not cops.'

The vagrant looked at the fifteen pounds. 'Make it twenty.'

Shack added another tenner. 'Let's call it twenty five, eh?'

The guy flashed a yellow-toothed smile. 'I was here that night. Bloody cops everywhere. I buggered off before they saw me. They pull you in for anything.'

'Quite right. Cops are a pain in the arse. But did you see anything of what happened?'

The man looked up and down the street. 'There were three of them. A woman and two men. Came outta there.' He pointed to the club door. 'The men had hold of her. They started knocking her about. I heard her scream, so I fucked off. When I came back the place was swarming with the filth.'

'Two men? You sure?'

'Yeah, I'm sure. Now can I get my money?'

Shack handed over the notes. 'If we needed to talk to you again, how can we get hold of you?'

The man made to leave again. 'Forget that shit. I'm not getting involved.'

'There'll be a couple of hundred in it for you.'

He turned. 'Two hundred?'

'Maybe more. What's your name?'

'They call me, Chalky, Chalky White.'

'Okay, Chalky, and where can we find you?'

The guy was quiet for a few moments. 'Okay. My usual beat is Piccadilly Circus or Trafalgar Square. Most nights I sleep down there.'

'Good. Cheers, mate.' Shack took a business card from his wallet and handed it to the guy. 'If you need to contact me here's my number.'

The vagrant looked at the card and grinned. 'Right I'll just pop this number into my latest iPhone, eh?'

Shack smiled at the irony. 'Yeah, okay, mate. You take care now, Chalky.'

They watched as he shuffled off into the darkness. 'Really?' said Amanda.

'Really what?'

'You going to believe that poor soul? He'd have told you anything to get a few pounds.'

Shack took her arm and moved her across to the other side of the street. 'Look.' He pointed to three CCTV cameras. 'They're covering the back of the club, that door and that end of the alley. But not this side of the street. These lights shine mostly on this side of the street. Old Chalky would be able to see everything on this side.'

'So?'

'So why would he say two men came out with Samantha? You said the inside CCTV showed her going out of the club with one man. Nothing from the external coverage. Correct?'

'Yes.'

'And definitely nothing about two men.'

'Definitely not.'

He nodded towards the cameras. 'There must be footage somewhere from those.'

'I think it would've been wiped by now, Shack.'

'Probably from the in-house hard-drive. But those are Sentinel Security's cameras.'

'Sentinel? The company your sleazebag friend owns?'

'The very same.'

'Okay.'

'And as far as I remember, Sentinel always backed up their CCTV footage onto the Cloud.'

'But wouldn't the police have known that and asked to see it?'

'Maybe. Maybe not. I'm banking on not. And I'll bet our friend Donny still has that footage on file. And I'll bet that footage is how he got the money to buy Sentinel.'

'So, how do we get hold of it?'

He looked at her for several seconds, then said. 'I have no idea . . . yet!'

'What now?'

He offered her his arm. 'Back to Hammersmith.'

She linked her arm through his. 'So, no more clubbing then?'

'Not tonight, Y'Ladyship.'

In the top floor office of *Idols*, Donny Black stood in front of several CCTV monitors. He watched as Shack and Amanda walked out of view. Then said quietly, 'Now what the fuck are you up to Bobby boy?'

Chapter Sixteen
'A Very Nice Macon'

It is no accident the Masonic Hall on Belvedere Road boasts more members from the Metropolitan Police, and Parliament, than any other in the UK. Located opposite Jubilee Gardens, on the south side of the Thames, it's only minutes from Scotland Yard or the Palace of Westminster. Indeed, any of its rooms that look onto the river, have clear sight of both paragons of justice and democracy.

There are several lodges that use Belvedere Road, the most prestigious being *The Knights' Lodge*, which usually meets every other Tuesday. The Hall itself is open every day and has an excellent restaurant, serving breakfast, lunch and dinner. There is also accommodation for those who may require it. Being Saturday, there were not as many members in the building as on a weekday.

There were however two distinguished masons, from the Knights' Lodge, taking lunch, Sir Anthony Fairfax, a senior civil servant in the House of Lords and Thomas Morrison, Deputy Commander, National Crime Agency.

They watched in silence as the Maître d' expertly filleted their Dover Sole. After serving them, he said, 'Anything else, gentlemen?'

Sir Anthony shook his head. 'Thank you, Stephen.' He picked up his wineglass and sniffed at the contents. 'This is a very nice Macon. Cheers, Tom.'

Morrison took a sip of wine. 'Yes. Cheers.'

'So, what's so important you drag me into the city on such a lovely Saturday?'

'We have a problem.'

Sir Anthony swallowed a mouthful of fish, then wiped his lips. 'We?'

'Yes, Anthony. We.'

'Lower your voice, man. Now what is the issue?'

The Commander leaned forward. 'Robert Stone.'

'I'm sorry, Tom, you'll have to remind me.'

'The detective from Islington. The car accident. His wife was killed. He survived.'

Sir Anthony frowned. 'Ah yes. That little project didn't quite work out as was planned. But he did go to prison, I believe.'

'That's right.'

'So, what exactly is your problem, Tom?'

'Our problem, Sir Anthony . . . *our problem.* Stone is out and back in London. He was in *Idols* last night.'

'Doing what, exactly?'

'He was in the club. And then seen at the rear of the place. Had a woman with him.'

'Really? He went to a night club. Had a drink. With a woman. Then went out the back. Goodness me. How surprising.'

'This is no joking matter!'

'Oh, I never joke, Tom. I'm a civil servant. I have no sense of humour. Now will you please get to the point.'

Morrison took a mouthfull of wine. 'He's sniffing around.'

'Sniffing around? What on earth does that mean?'

'We think it could be to do with the Osborne woman.'

'I'm sorry? Who?'

'Samantha Osborne. The woman who was killed at the back of *Idols*.'

Sir Anthony put his cutlery down and wiped his lips. 'Ah, yes. A strikingly good looking girl as I recall. Such a waste. I understand she'd become quite an issue.'

'Err, yes. You could say that. She was onto several elements of our organization.'

'So, what's the connection between Robert Stone and the recently departed Miss Osborne?'

'We don't know yet.'

'Then I suggest you find out. And smartly, Tom. Or there'll be larger issues to deal with. And some very unhappy people.'

Chapter Seventeen
'Dragon Boats'

In Hammersmith, Shack and Amanda were on the balcony reading the Saturday papers. The sun was warm, so she'd pulled down the canopy for some welcome shade. Lunch had been a sandwich and a beer for Shack, a salad for her. They'd spoken at length about the previous night's sortie to *Idols* and the mood although sombre, was positive.

'I know we can't get Samantha's info until Monday, but do you feel up to talking about her now?'

She put the paper down. 'Yes, of course. We both need to know what happened to Sam and Chrissy, no matter how painful.'

'You mind if I get another beer?'

'No. Help yourself. Could you bring me some water, please?'

A few moments later her returned with the drinks. 'What's this?' he said, as he pointed to the river.

She stood up and smiled. 'Oh, yes. They practice every Saturday. Dragon Boat racers.'

'That's so cool.'

They watched in silence as the two longboats, each with a dragon figurehead passed her building. The crews all rowed in unison. Their hypnotic chant, to keep them in time, drifted across the water to the watchers on each side of the river.

'Dragon Boats on the Thames. Very cool,' said Shack.

They sat back down under the canopy. 'This is one hot summer,' said Amanda.

Shack took a swallow of his beer. 'Ain't that the truth. So, did Sam talk much about what she was doing?'

'Not at first, but then she realized what was happening. We spoke a lot as she became more involved. She wasn't supposed to, but what the hell, I wasn't going to betray her confidence. They had her sign the Official Secrets Act you know. When she told me that, I knew it was more serious than she initially imagined.'

'How did she get involved? You mentioned she wasn't with the police, so how did they recruit her?'

'She worked in Westminster. She was always interested in politics. At college she was president of the debating society.'

'So you knew her from university?'

Amanda smiled, then shook her head slightly. 'Oh, no. She was up at Oxford. I went to Edinburgh. We met about six years ago, when I was doing a piece for the Guardian. She was at the Foreign Office. Principal Personal Secretary to the Minister of State.'

'Wow. Impressive.'

'She was an impressive woman.'

Shack smiled. 'I'm sure.'

'One evening Sam came back and said she'd had a meeting with the Home Secretary. She, the Home Secretary that is, was a friend of Samantha's mother. So there was a family connection which was probably the reason the Home Secretary wanted to recruit her.'

'Right, okay.'

'At that meeting the Home Secretary had spoken briefly about her plans for Overwatch. It was to infiltrate various elements of the government, the judiciary and the police, and expose the connections with organised crime across the UK.'

'So, Sam agreed?'

'Not at first. The Home Secretary was going to be out of the country for a couple of days, so Sam had a little time to consider. We spoke about it and, to be honest, I was against it. I said it may turn out to be a lot more dangerous than she thought.'

'What did she say?'

'She promised to be careful and not do anything to put herself in danger. Look how that turned out.'

Shack saw the tears well up. 'You want to stop?'

She shook her head, then wiped her eyes. 'But after a couple of days she said she felt she had to do something that had meaning. She was read-in to the whole Overwatch project about a year ago.'

'Right . . . and what she discovered is now safely stored in the deposit box?'

'Yes. We'll go to the bank first thing Monday morning.'

'Great. I'm gonna have another beer, okay?'

'Sure, mi casa es su casa.'

'Oh, you speak Chinese?'

'It's Spanish. It means . . .'

He grinned. 'I'm kidding, Y'Ladyship.'

She smiled. 'Right. I'll have a beer as well, please.'

* * *

It was late Saturday afternoon when, Deputy Commander, Thomas Morrison got home. His wife was unhappy at his late arrival. They were going to a friend's

67

barbecue at six and she needed to pick up several items from the supermarket before then. 'Where have you been, Tom? It's after five.'

'Sorry darling. The meeting went on longer than I expected.'

'Well hurry up and change. We should still be okay for six.'

Morrison smiled, then kissed her cheek. He trotted up the stairs, and called back, 'Ready in fifteen minutes.' As he undressed, his phone beeped. He looked at the screen and frowned. 'Yes?'

'Hello, Commander. We've managed to trace Robert Stone, sir. He is living in Manchester, as we thought.'

'It's taken you all day to discover that?'

'It wasn't that straightforward, sir.'

'Get to the point.'

'He'd changed his name after leaving prison. He now calls himself Shackleton Blister.'

Morrison laughed. 'Are you serious? Shackleton Blister?'

'Absolutely, sir. It's all been done legally. Not just a cover name.'

'Right. You have an address?'

'Yes, sir.'

'Okay. Go and check the place out. I'm told he's here in London now, so it should be a simple enough task for you northern idiots to get in without being discovered.'

'Very good, sir. We'll be in touch.' The line went silent. The northern idiot looked at the blank screen and sneered, 'Wanker.'

Chapter Eighteen
'Candid Camera'

Shack and Amanda had spent the day talking and drinking beers. By ten o'clock they had finished their Indian takeaway. 'I'm going to be like the side of a house before this is all over,' said Amanda.'

He frowned. 'What?'

'All this food and beer. You're a bad influence, Mr B. I'm going to have to work twice as hard in the gym tomorrow.'

Shack raised his beer bottle. 'You look pretty good to me, Y'Ladyship.'

'Yeah, but you can only see me with one eye…Oh, I'm sorry! What an awful thing to say.'

He scowled at her for a few seconds, then laughed out loud. 'Yeah, but very funny.'

She shook her head. 'I'll get a couple more beers, then I'm off to bed.'

He gave a thumbs-up, as he finished off his drink. 'I might have a shot of that Macallan as well, if that's okay?'

* * *

The next morning, Amanda woke to the sound of a phone beeping. She looked at the bedside clock; a quarter to nine. The beeping continued. She got up and slipped on a robe, then went into the drawing room. Shack's phone lay on the floor, its ring-tone increasing in volume. He was on the couch, totally oblivious to the irritating device. The empty bottle of Macallan lay on the floor next to him.

Amanda picked up the phone then shook him hard. 'Hey.' No response. The smell of whisky was overpowering. She slapped his face, and shouted, 'Shack.'

He opened his eye. 'What the fuck?'

'Your phone. It's been ringing for ages.'

'Oh . . . Sorry.' He looked at the screen, then swiped it. 'Ruby?'

'Shack, hi, baby. Are you okay? Did I wake you?'

He sat up. 'No, I'm okay, gorgeous. Whatsup?'

'I got a call from your building supervisor. He said he couldn't get through to you and my number was down as an alternative.'

'Oh . . . Yeah, right. I had to put someone down and yours was all I could think of. Sorry.'

'It's okay. I'm pleased you'd think of me. Anyway . . . I'm in your office. It's been broken into.' The line was silent for several seconds. 'Shack? You there?'

'Yeah, sorry. I'm here.'

'They've turned the place over pretty good. Your flat in the back as well.'

'Okay. Listen, Ruby, can you get the office secure, please? Not that there's anything in there worth stealing.'

'The supervisor's repairing the door as we speak. He said you'll need to pay for the damage.'

'Yeah, that's okay. I'll sort him out when I get back.'

'Are you coming back?'

'Not just yet, love. I've still things to do down here.'

'Okay. Anything else you need me to do?'

'No, thanks. You've been a great help. You're a star, babe.'

'Anytime. Listen, you look after yourself, Shack. I might not be a detective, but I know offices don't get broken into for no reason.'

He smiled at the sound of the kisses. 'Thanks, gorgeous. I'll be in touch. Bye.'

* * *

In Shack's office the supervisor continued to whinge as he replaced the broken lock. Once finished, he handed Ruby a new set of keys. 'There'll be a service charge as well as the repairs, tell him.'

She smiled and held out a tenner. 'I will. And thank you.'

He looked at the note. 'Err, you don't need to do that, love.'

'Don't be silly. Get yourself a pint.'

He stuffed the money in his pocket and grinned. 'Okay, cheers.'

After he left, she went into the back living area again and looked around. 'Oh, Shack. You can do better than this, baby.' She locked up and took the lift to the ground floor. On her way out she passed through the reception area.

The supervisor waved from his office. 'Bye.'

She raised her hand. 'Thanks again.'

As she backed her car out of the visitor parking, a dark blue Audi started its engine. She drove onto the main road and switched on Radio Manchester. Beyoncé was belting out *Single Ladies*. Ruby joined in.

The same song filled the blue Audi; two cars behind her.

Ruby pulled into the underground parking of her building, a little after 10am. As she got out of her car, the blue Audi stopped in front of hers. Two men stepped out. The bigger of the two smiled. 'Hi there.'

She frowned. 'Can I help you?'

'Yes, please. We're trying to contact a Robert Michael Stone.'

'No, sorry. You should ask at the concierge desk. They know all the residents.' The smaller of the two said, 'You probably know him as Shackleton Blister.'

Ruby shook her head and smiled. 'Sorry, I don't know that name. Ask at the desk.'

'Really? . . . So why have you just spent an hour at his office in Salford Quays?'

She tried to pass them, but the big man grabbed her arm. 'Hang on, love.'

The spray hissed from the container; the Mace blinded him. 'Ahhh! You, fucking bitch.'

The smaller took hold of her. 'Nice one, love. You're under arrest for assaulting a police officer.'

She struggled. 'Police? You never said you were police.'

'Doesn't matter, you just assaulted my colleague here.'

She tried to free herself. 'Not before he grabbed me.'

The man smirked. 'Yeah, well, no one's gonna believe that are they?'

She stopped struggling and pointed to the ceiling. 'Oh, I think they will.'

The man looked up at the CCTV camera.

'Smile,' said Ruby, 'you're on Candid Camera.'

The man released her, and she rushed to the lift. She hit the button and, as she stepped in, the big man shouted, 'We'll be seeing you soon. Bitch.'

Before the lift doors closed, she shouted back, 'Not with those eyes. Arsehole.'

Chapter Nineteen
'Someone's Worried'

After the call with Ruby, Shack went to his room and showered. When he returned Amanda was on the balcony reading the paper. There was a pot of tea and several slices of toast on the table.

'Good morning,' she said, 'how are you feeling? You want some breakfast?'

'Mornin.' He sat down. 'Tea n' toast will do me thanks. Sorry about earlier.'

She smiled at the sheepish look on his face. 'It's fine. You were out for the count though.'

He swallowed a mouthful of tea. 'Err, yeah, we did have a few beers yesterday.'

She lowered her head and looked over the top of her spectacles. 'Not to mention the best part of a bottle of Macallan.'

He adjusted the eye patch. 'Err, yes. That too I suppose. I'll replace that.'

'Don't be silly. You'd better eat something.'

He smiled, then spread a film of honey over a piece of toast.

She put the paper down. 'Everything okay? With the phone call I mean.'

He wiped his mouth. 'My office was broken into.'

'Really? That's not good.'

'There's nothing in there worth stealing. But . . .'

'I didn't mean that,' she interrupted, 'my point was why now?'

He sipped some more tea. 'Exactly. I was just about to say the same thing.'

Amanda leaned forward. 'So, someone is worried?'

He nodded. 'There are only two people know I'm down here.'

'The sleazy doorman at Idols?'

'Yes. And my friend Ruby in Manchester. And she's not going to tell anyone.'

His phone beeped. He dashed back into the drawing room. 'Hi, gorgeous. You okay?'

'Yes. I'm fine, baby. But just had a problem with a couple of cops. Well, they said they were police, but I never hung around to see any warrant cards.'

'Are you all right?'

'Yes. Yes, I'm fine. They were asking about you, Shack. They must have been watching me in your office. What the hell's going on?'

'It's a long story. Listen, just stay away from my place for the foreseeable. Okay? And take care.'

'Am I in danger?'

'No. Definitely not. It's me they're looking for. Just be extra careful who you're dealing with for a while.'

'Okay. Are you sure you're alright, Shack?'

'Yeah. I'm with a friend down here, so don't worry.'

'If you say so . . . You take care too. I don't want anything to happen to you, baby.'

'Thanks, gorgeous. Bye.'

The line went silent.

Back on the balcony, Amanda said, 'More trouble?'

He went to the rail and looked out across the Thames. 'Yes. A couple of cops spoke to Ruby. Asking about me.'

'Is she alright?'

'I think they upset her more than she's saying. But she's a tough lady and yes, she's fine.'

She joined him at the handrail. 'So, we have definitely got someone worried.'

He nodded. 'Yes. And that's good. Because if they're worried, they'll start to make mistakes. And we can play against their weakness.'

'Do we know their weakness?'

'We do. Their arrogance and their ego. They think they're fireproof.'

'But we are going to burn them down. Right, partner?'

'You bet your perfect arse we are, Y'Ladyship. How do you fancy a beer over in Islington?'

'What?'

'A Sunday afternoon drink in Islington.'

She shook her head. 'I'm not drinking today. And I need to get to the gym this afternoon.'

'Go do your gym thing now, if you must. But we need to go to my old local in Islington.'

'Ah, so, it's not just another day boozing.'

He grinned. 'As if?'

'Right. I'll do an hour downstairs, then we can drive over there about one-ish?'

'No need to drive. We'll take the tube.'

'I'm not drinking. So, I can drive us. And the Sunday traffic should be okay.'

'It's not that. Best not to give anyone a car reg they can check.' He winked. 'You'll be Caroline again, if need be.'

'Right . . . Caroline, and the tube, it is.'

Chapter Twenty
'Sunday Golf'

On the third tee, at *Wentworth Golf Club*, Lord Edward Valentine had just hit a two-hundred and twenty yard drive.

'Excellent shot, sir,' said Sir Anthony Fairfax.

'Yes indeed. Great drive, sir,' said Deputy Commander Thomas Morrison.

Valentine nodded as he slipped the driver into his golf bag. 'Yes, that was rather good.'

The three climbed aboard the buggy and set off down the cart-way. In the rear seat   Morrison's phone vibrated. He took it out and looked at the screen. 'Sorry, gentlemen. I really need to take this.'

Sir Anthony shot Morrison a withering look. His Lordship was more intent on speeding the buggy to his next shot.

Morrison spoke quietly. A few words later, and the call ended. He looked at the device and waited for the incoming message. The phone pinged. A disdainful look from Fairfax was met with another, 'Sorry,' from Morrison. He flicked through the message as the buggy came to a stop.

'Your honour, I think, Thomas,' said Valentine.

Morrison hit a seven iron onto the green, and the round continued.

Later, in the elegant clubhouse, the three went out to the patio and watched the golfers come up the eighteenth.

Having arrived in his chauffeured Bentley, Valentine and Fairfax were able to enjoy a very nice bottle of Nuit-Saint-Georges. Morrison, unfortunately, sipped at his pint of orange juice.

'So, what was so urgent about your call, Tom?' said Sir Anthony.

'Oh, I can fill you in later, sir.'

'I hope it's nothing we should be worried about, Tom,' added Valentine.

'Just something up in Manchester, sir.'

'Manchester, Tom. Might that be to do with our friend Mr Shackleton Blister?' said Fairfax.

'Yes, sir. Well, not directly.'

His Lordship chuckled. 'Shackleton Blister? What a splendid name. Positively Dickensian. And who might he be?'

'Someone we've been looking into, Lord Valentine,' said Morrison. 'You'll probably remember him as Robert Michael Stone, sir. The detective we . . .'

Valentine's smile turned to a deep frown. 'I know who you mean, Thomas. I thought we had dealt with him?'

Morrison nodded. 'Yes, sir. But not as we wanted. He's been off the grid for some time. But we've recently flagged him as a possible issue.'

Valentine took another sip of Burgundy. 'A possible issue? Which brings us back to your phone call, Thomas?'

Morrison took out his phone and swiped the screen. 'We had a look over his office in Manchester. Nothing of any significance. But there was a woman there. Our men had a brief word with her.'

'A brief word, Tom? Was that necessary?' said Fairfax.

Morrison disregarded the jibe and continued. 'We believe she's a friend of Stone's . . . Blister's.' He looked at the screen. 'Ruby Teresa Brennan. Thirty-three. Born in Leeds. Jamaican mother, British father. Graduated Leeds University, with a first in psychology. Moved to Manchester ten years ago. Owns several properties in the city. Self-employed.'

'Self-employed as what?' said Fairfax.

'She's an escort, sir.' Morrison passed his phone to Sir Anthony. 'This is her.'

Fairfax looked at the photo, then handed the phone to his Lordship.

'Goodness me,' said Valentine. 'What a fine looking filly. Wouldn't mind a canter with her myself.'

Morrison took the phone and, continuing the equestrian thread, said, 'I think you may find she's a trifle spirited, sir. She sprayed one of my men with Mace!'

Chapter Twenty One
'A Pirate'

The Boatman hotel overlooks the Regents Canal in the heart of Islington. On a Sunday the place is busy with regular customers from all over the borough, who come to enjoy the excellent lunch it serves.

Amanda had worked-out for over an hour and a half. The Underground journey had taken a little over twenty minutes, and the short walk from Angel tube station to the pub, another ten minutes. It was almost two o'clock when they entered *The Boatman*.

Shack wiped the sweat from his forehead and adjusted the eyepatch. 'I'm choking for a pint What do you want, love?'

'A large lime and soda, please. Lots of ice.'

At the bar a young woman came over. 'Yes, sir?'

Shack asked for the drinks and dropped a tenner on the counter.

When the drinks arrived, the barmaid said, 'Are you having lunch, sir?'

He shook his head and smiled. 'Just these for now, thanks.'

Amanda swallowed a third of her drink. 'So, no tinted glasses today?'

He fiddled with the patch again. 'No need. This used to be mine and Chrissy's local. There'll be people in here who know me.'

She nodded and took another drink. 'But they'll know you as Robert Stone, not Shack.'

'Yeah.'

She smiled. 'You never did tell me why you picked that name.'

'I used to write short stories in prison. Shackleton Blister was the name of a character. A butler, actually. Just stuck in my head.'

'Ah, I see. Well I think it's a marvellous name. Cheers.'

'Yeah, I believe you, Y'Ladyship.'

'So, why are we here, partner?'

'A few of the detectives I worked with at Islington get in now and again. Thought we might be able to pick up,,,'

'Bob?'

Shack turned to the bar. 'Hello, Brian. How've you been?'

They shook hands, the barman clearly shocked at Shack's appearance. 'Jesus, mate what the hell happened to you?'

'Long story, Bri. Was in an accident a few years back.'

'Yes, yes. I read about it. Car crash. Chrissy was killed. Oh, Jesus, I didn't mean to blurt it out like that.'

'It's okay, was a while ago now.'

'The bloody papers said you were over the limit. Which I thought was strange. And the bastards gave y'time for manslaughter. As if losing Chrissy and the baby wasn't bad enough.'

'Yeah, it was a bad time . . . What do you mean, strange?'

'About the drink driving. Them saying you were over the limit. Coz I remember when y'found out she was expecting, y'stopped drinkin as well.'

Shack nodded. 'Yeah, that's right.'

A customer shouted for an order. Brian raised his hand in acknowledgment, then turned to Shack. 'Hey look, I really am so sorry, mate. Chrissy was a wonderful girl. Scuse me.'

Amanda watched as Shack quickly wiped a tear from his eye. She linked her arm through his. 'Let's go find a seat outside,' she said.

It was busier outside than in, with everyone wanting to get their share of the afternoon sun. A couple of narrow boats, negotiating a passing manoeuvre, provided further entertainment for the diners and drinkers. A table at the far side of the frontage was vacant and they quickly took seats in the shade of a large willow.

'This is really nice here, Shack. You must have been happy here?'

'Yeah. We had a nice house two blocks away.' He pointed across the water. 'On the other side of the canal. 'Lost that of course, when I went inside.'

She touched his hand, then leaned forward. 'Brian, the barman, said you had decided to abstain for the duration of the pregnancy?'

He gave a little laugh. 'Yeah. I promised Chrissy, if she wasn't able to have a drink, I'd do the same.'

'That's good. And why not? Us girls always get the short end.'

'Ain't that the truth.' He stood up. 'You want another drink?'

'Yes, please. I'll have the same.'

'Anything to eat?'

'No, I'm fine till we get home. But you get something if you want.'

He came out with the drinks. As he passed a nearby table, a little boy looked at him and said excitedly, 'Mummy, mummy, a pirate!'

The embarrassed mother pulled the child to her. 'Timothy. That's very rude.' Then to Shack. 'I'm so sorry.'

Shack shook his head. 'It's okay.' Then he leaned down to the boy and said 'Arrrrrr!'

Amanda smiled as the giggling Timothy watched the pirate walk away.

When he sat down, Amanda said, 'You made his day.'

'Kids eh . . . Cheers.'

She took the straw and stirred the ice around, then looked him in the eye. 'So, you weren't drinking when the accident happened?'

He put his pint down, then shook his head. 'Nope.'

'So how could you possibly be over the limit?'

'Exactly.'

'You feel like talking about the accident?'

He was quiet for several seconds, his gaze on the water. He took a drink. 'She loved it here. You wouldn't think this was London.'

Amanda smiled. 'It is very nice. And not on the tourist map.'

'Yeah. It's nice.' He turned to her and leaned forward. 'We'd just been for the three months scan. The medical centre not far from here. Chrissy was so happy. It was a girl you know . . . Would have been a girl.'

She smiled again and nodded.

'I was about to turn into our avenue . . . The van came from nowhere. Hit us head-on. Our car was thrown back and into a parked car.' He took another drink. 'I was out

83

for a few seconds, but came round quickly, probably adrenalin fuelled.'

Again, she nodded.

'The front of the car was on fire; the interior filling with smoke. My door was buckled but I kicked it open. Flames were coming from the footwell. I tried to get her door open . . . it was buckled worse than mine. Ran back to my side . . . tried to get her across the centre-column.' He shook his head. 'Flames . . . flames were strong. Burning . . . Smoke . . . Burning. I couldn't breathe. They said later my lungs had been scorched. Someone pulled me out as the interior went up . . . I don't remember anything after that. I was out of it for a couple of days. They induced a coma so they could treat these.' He held up his hands. 'When I came out of it, they told me she was gone. As if I didn't know that. Said she wouldn't have felt anything.'

She put her hand on his. 'That's enough, Shack.'

He shook his head and sucked in a deep breath. 'It was a couple of days later, even before I left the hospital, the police said I was being charged with DUI. I didn't understand it . . . Thought it was some mistake, some test issue. The rest is public knowledge. History.'

'And the van driver. Just disappeared; I believe?'

'Yeah. Hit n'run, as they say . . . Hit and run.'

Amanda stood up. 'My round. Same again?'

He nodded, then looked out across the canal. 'Same again. Always same again.'

As she walked to the bar, she wiped the tears from her eyes.

Chapter Twenty Two
'Box 107'

The overnight temperatures made for an uncomfortable and muggy Sunday night. Monday morning however, brought a mild northerly breeze that freshened the day. Amanda had made a couple of bacon baguettes and breakfast, looking out over the Thames, was a pleasant start to the day.

With her bank in the centre of the city, it made sense to take the tube instead of the car and they arrived at the bank a little after eleven.

Amanda was welcomed by the Deposit Facility Manager. 'Good morning, Miss Lang, nice to see you again.'

'Morning. Before we go down, I'd like this gentleman included on the access protocol, please.'

'Certainly, madam. This way, please.'

As the three walked towards the private office, Shack leaned forward. 'You want to give me access?'

'Yes. If anything happens to me, you will still be able to use what's in the box.'

He leaned closer. 'Nothing is gonna' happen to you, Y'Ladyship.'

Several minutes later, they were in the secure deposit vault. The facility manager tapped in the bank's code. Box 107's keypad turned from red to amber.

He smiled. 'If I can help further, madam, please let me know.'

'Thank you.'

After he'd gone, Amanda tapped in her code. The keypad turned green and the door clicked open. She pulled out the internal container. Shack followed her to one of the small side rooms.

As she sat down, she took a deep breath. 'Okay, Samantha, my darling . . . '

He sat alongside her. 'You okay? I can do this.'

She nodded. 'I'm fine, really. I've been through it before, but you need to see it, and perhaps make more of it than I?'

The box contained several documents, some photographs, and a hard drive. Amanda took an ipad from her handbag and attached the drive. As she brought up the information, Shack looked through the documents, two of which were photocopies of newspaper articles.

He held them up. 'So, this is how you found me?'

She looked over the top of her spectacles and nodded. 'Yes.'

'The article about the crash. And the other about the court case.'

Without looking up, she said again, 'Yes.'

'That's impressive detective work, Amanda.'

She turned the ipad towards him. 'What do you make of this?'

He read through the information, scrolling down as he did so. 'This is great work. Samantha was really at the heart of what was happening.'

'Unfortunately, yes . . .'

'Oh, I'm sorry. I didn't mean to be insensitive . . . It's just . . .'

'It's okay, Shack. Really.'

He looked at the screen. 'Senior Police and Government Ministers in league with organised crime. Drug money being rinsed through immigrant operated businesses, car-washes.' He looked at her. 'I was working on a big money-laundering case. East European cash businesses.' He tapped the screen. 'Especially bloody car-washes.'

She took off her glasses and leaned forward. 'And that is why they wanted you out of the way, partner.'

Chapter Twenty Three
'The Red Queen'

Poland's accession to the European Union in the summer of 2004, opened the gates to the first wave of Polish immigrants to the UK. One of the first to arrive was the Stavos family. Roman and his flame-haired wife, Lena, both in their mid-thirties, arrived with their son, Micha. After renting a tiny two-room flat in the suburbs of London, it was only a matter of weeks until Roman Stavos had set up one of the first immigrant operated car-wash services in Britain.

By Christmas 2014, Roman had established over two-thousand such businesses across the UK, most of which were in London, Birmingham and Manchester. Their tiny rented home was a far cry from the multi-million pound Buckinghamshire stud-farm the family now owned.

The Stavos's success, to all intents and purposes, looked like the realisation of the immigrant's dream. Work hard and all you desire can be yours. In truth, Roman Stavos had been a small time gangster in his hometown of Tarnów, south east Poland and coming to England had been a necessity, after a *Śmierć jakikolwiek sposób* contract -*Death by any means*- had been taken out on him.

On Christmas Day 2014, after ten years in the UK, that contract was fulfilled. A bomb, in the form of a Christmas gift, had exploded in the family home. Roman, and his son Micha were killed immediately. But Lena survived unharmed and lived to take over the business.

Lena Stavos carried on her husband's legacy, becoming one of the most ruthless people in the world of organised crime. Her long fiery locks became a focus for those who dealt with her. She was known, by friends and foes alike, as *The Red Queen.*

The Bentley came to a stop in front of the enormous house. The chauffeur quickly opened the door and Lord Edward Valentine stepped out. He looked at the huge pile and shook his head. 'Could this place be any more vulgar?'

'My Lord?' said the chauffeur.

Valentine held up his hand. 'Just thinking out loud, Colin.'

'Yes, My Lord.'

Valentine quickly swapped his frown for a charm-filled smile, as Lena Stavos appeared. 'Lord Valentine. How lovely to see you again.'

'Lena . . . Looking wonderful as always, my dear.'

She smiled. 'Come in, come in.'

The interior of the house, although clearly filled with expensive furniture, was as tasteless as the exterior. Lena Stavos however was an entirely different matter. She was beautiful and, at almost fifty, looked ten years younger. Edward Valentine had always been attracted to the woman and since her husband's demise, the relationship between The Red Queen and the Peer of the Realm had become decidedly more intimate.

The feelings Lena had for Valentine were not at all on the same plane as the lord's. She knew he needed her more than she needed him. Their business dealings however were mutually dependant so the occasional sexual encounter, though not unpleasant, ensured she maintained the upper hand. But today, sadly for his Lordship, there would be no such encounter.

'So, Edward. To what do we owe this unexpected pleasure?'

Valentine swirled the cognac around in the balloon. He inhaled the heady aroma, then swallowed a mouthful of the amber liquid. 'Mmmm. Excellent.'

'Edward?'

'Yes, yes. Sorry, my dear. Yes, we seem to have a little problem.'

Chapter Twenty Four
'An Elegant Set-up'

Shack and Amanda left the bank a little before one o'clock. 'Mind if we have a walk?' she said.

'Yeah, why not. You sure you're okay?'

She linked her arm though his and smiled. 'Yes, it's just seeing those things. Sam's way of doing things. How she was so meticulous.'

He squeezed her arm in his. 'I get it, love. You hungry?'

'Not really. You?'

'No, but maybe we can stop for a drink somewhere?'

'Sure. But let's walk a little first. I really need some air.'

After twenty minutes they found themselves at the river, across from the Houses of Parliament.

'Here,' said Shack. 'Let's have a seat.'

The shade from the trees was welcome. He took out a handkerchief, lifted the eye-patch and wiped the sweat from his face. The Embankment was busy with tourists walking, smiling, taking pictures.

'It's got to be twenty-eight degrees. How come you look so cool, Y'Ladyship?'

She smiled, then said in an overly posh voice, 'Oh, we in the aristocracy are not allowed to perspire, my good man.'

He laughed. 'Yeah, just us riff-raff do that.'

A small group of Japanese stopped in front of them. Chattering excitedly, they pointed to the Parliament building, then snapped away with their cameras and phones. One of them realised they were blocking Shack and Amanda's view. He bowed slightly. 'Solly, solly.' Then moved his group a little farther down the pathway.

Shack stood and offered her his arm. 'Time for a beer I think?'

She linked her arm through his, then nodded towards the road. 'There's a nice little place up here.'

The front of the restaurant overlooked the river and was, unsurprisingly, full. The young Italian waiter, who was clearly taken with Amanda, suggested they go through to the rear garden. A few minutes later he appeared at their table with drinks

'One beer for sir. Lime and soda,' he smiled at Amanda, 'with lots of ice, for madam. Enjoy.'

Shack tapped his glass against hers. 'Cheers.' He swallowed half the contents, then grinned. 'Oh . . . I needed that.'

The enclosed garden was a little humid but, as they had shade, bearable. Amanda leaned forward and said quietly. 'So, what do you make of it all, Detective Blister?'

He finished his pint, then waved the empty glass at the young waiter. 'Same again please, son.'

The Italian nodded and went inside.

'First off, I don't understand why the Home Secretary hasn't got all that info? Why didn't Samantha pass it on?'

'She did pass-on her initial findings. But after she was killed, I felt I needed to find who was responsible and took the decision not to surrender the information. I'd seen the news pieces about you and thought we might be able to help each other. That was about six weeks ago. It took me a little time to find you . . . and here we are.'

The waiter arrived. 'One beer, sir.' He smiled at Amanda, 'Nothing for you, madam?'

She smiled and shook her head.

Shack swallowed a mouthfull. 'Okay, I understand that. And I think I understand the setup. It's extremely elegant.'

'I believe I do as well. But let's hear your theory, partner?'

He put his elbows on the table and leaned closer. 'We have the key players. Thomas Morrison, a Deputy Commander, in the NCA. Sir Anthony Fairfax, a senior civil servant, who appears to be the top gofer to this Lord Edward Valentine. And it looks clear enough, from Samantha's treasure, that Morrison has counterparts in Birmingham and Manchester and is controlling lesser police officers, mostly detectives, in those cities as well as here. Sir Anthony is, to my mind, the liaison between the police end of the syndicate and his master Lord Valentine.'

Amanda nodded. 'I agree.'

'Valentine has, it would appear, distanced himself from the day-to-day operation. But he seems to be the one closest to the colourfully named, Red Queen.'

Amanda nodded, clearly encourage by his understanding of the evidence. 'Yes. The Red Queen? . . . Oh, sorry, go on.'

He took another drink. 'As I said, it's a pretty elegant set up. Narcotics are coming into the country from Europe. Corrupt detectives turn a blind eye to eighty percent of the dealings. Twenty percent are discovered, with low level villains being charged and sentenced. This keeps up the appearance of sound policing. The money from the sale of the drugs, and any other business the syndicate is involved in, is then rinsed through a network of immigrant-operated businesses, mostly car-wash services.'

'Which is what you were investigating before they…'

'Yeah . . . The laundered money is then sent back to Europe, where it's moved on to various offshore bank accounts for the players to access. Like I said, a very elegant setup.'

'But there is nothing to give us any clue as to who killed Amanda, and set you up?'

'The police fitted me up. It must be. They're the only ones who could arrange for my alcohol test to be fixed as positive. It's not a difficult thing to do if you influence the right people. At the time I didn't know why they did it, but now it's crystal.'

'And Sam's killers? The two men Chalky White believes he saw? You think they were police?'

He shook his head. 'No. Definitely not. But I'm sure my old pal Donny Black got the money to buy his little company from the people who did kill her.'

'So, we need to get Mr Black to talk?'

'Yep.'

'And how do we do that?'

He finished his drink, and said, 'Right now, love, I have no idea.'

She frowned. 'What about The Red Queen? If the proceeds are laundered through immigrant businesses, maybe she's the brains behind that end of the operation?'

'Could be. We need to find the queen.'

'And we do that how? And please don't say, you have no idea.' She smiled at the hurt look on his face. 'Well?'

'That name came up a lot during my investigation into the rinsing operation.'

'So, you know who she is?'

'Hmm . . . Yeah. I think The Red Queen, could be a woman called Lena Stavos.'

Chapter Twenty Five
'Who's The Goat?'

Tuesday morning was overcast but, with temperatures in the high twenties, humid. Shack had answered several emails, one of which was a thank you from *Mr Brown*, then responded to several questions from Stella Davidson about her new recruits. She also confirmed the transfer of five thousand pounds to his account.

Amanda came in from the balcony. 'What are you smiling about?'

'Just got a few bob in in the bank. Will be able to pay the rent again.'

She sat down across from him. 'That always helps. So, you said it was time to up the game. How do we do that, partner?'

He closed the laptop. 'Did you see Jurassic Park?'

She frowned. 'Err, yes actually.'

'Remember the scene where the goat is staked out?'

'Yes. As bait for the T Rex.'

'Well that's the plan today.'

'Err, okay. So, who's going to be the goat. You or me?'

He winked. 'You're too valuable to be bait, Y'Ladyship.'

'I'd probably contest that but go on.'

'I'm going to the *Knights' Lodge* this evening.'

'The Knight's Lodge. Is that a pub?'

He laughed. 'Not really. It's the most prestigious lodge in the Belvedere Masonic Hall.'

'Ahh, the old secret society of Freemasons. Or as they prefer to say, society of secrets.'

* * *

Shack looked at his watch, almost eight o'clock. He'd been a Master Mason, for many years and had visited the Knight's Lodge a few times with police colleagues. He knew the chamber would be *close-tiled*, the masonic term for sealing the chamber, by eight pm. He trotted up the entrance steps and into the main hallway. A porter nodded, then watched him run up the elegant staircase.

The man at the chamber door looked stern. Formally dressed in an evening suit, he also wore an ornate apron and gauntlets. Around his neck hung a long Masonic chain. In his hand, a drawn sword.

Just as Shack arrived, the big oak door was slammed shut. The echo resonated through the building. The gatekeeper stood in front of him. 'Yes?'

'I am a brother from the East, travelling to the West.'

'And why do you make this journey?'

'To seek for that which was lost, and for the sake of the widow's son.'

The gatekeeper nodded seriously, then banged on the door with the hilt of his sword. A small hatch opened, and an equally serious man looked out. 'Who seeks to enter?'

The gatekeeper lowered his sword and stood to one side. 'Open, for a fellow Mason.'

The meeting closed at ten o'clock. Afterwards, most of the brothers adjourned to the *Belvedere Lounge* for a more cordial exchange. Shack had a drink with, and spoke to, several guys in the bar. None of which he knew. It was only as he was leaving, and thinking his idea was a washout, did one of the men approach. As they shook hands he said, 'Stephen Bowen.'

'Shackleton Blister. Call me Shack.'

Bowen smiled. 'Not seen you here before.'

'I'm just down for a couple of days. Thought I'd catch a meeting.'

'Down?'

'From Manchester. But I used to live and work in London.'

'Oh, yes?'

'Yeah, I was a detective, over at Islington.'

Bowen nodded. 'Ah, right. I thought you looked familiar. I'm across the river at the Met. Detective Inspector. So, are you still with the force?'

'Not now . . . Private.'

'Really? Interesting.' Bowen frowned. 'I do recognise you, but not the name.'

'I changed that when I came out of prison.'

'Prison?'

'Yeah. Had a crash. Was over the limit. Banged up.'

'Right . . . And you didn't get any help with that from the brothers in the force?'

Shack grinned. 'Quite the opposite actually.'

'Oh? How do you mean?'

'Long story, Steve. You want another drink?'

'No better not. Driving. And I'd better get off actually.'

Shack offered his hand. 'Okay, was good to meet you, brother.'

'You too, Shack. Good night.'

Shack finished his pint, then went to the bar and ordered a large malt.

Outside, DI Stephen Bowen was on his phone. 'Yes, it's him . . . Okay . . . I will . . . Bye.'

Shack downed his malt, then nodded a goodnight to the few remaining drinkers. In the hallway he removed his tie and stuffed it in his pocket, just as his phone beeped an incoming text. He swiped the screen, then frowned. *Don't go back to Hammersmith you are being followed.*

Chapter Twenty Six
'Sorry Chalky'

Once outside, he called Amanda. 'Shack, hi. Are you okay?'

'I'm fine, love. But just had a strange text.'

'Strange? From whom?'

'No idea. That's what makes it strange.'

'Saying what exactly?'

'That I'm being followed and not to go back to Hammersmith!' The line went quiet for several seconds. 'Amanda?'

'Yes, I'm here. So, whoever sent that knows about me.'

'Yes, but if they are warning me, that suggests they are probably friends.'

'I suppose so. But who?'

'Listen, don't worry. I'm outside the *Belvedere* and don't see anyone who looks suspicious. For the moment that is.'

'For the moment?'

'Listen, I'll have a bit of a wander, see if anyone sticks out. Might even check-in somewhere, and, if I am being tailed, it will give them a long night hanging around.'

'So, you're not coming back tonight?'

'Might be smart not to, love. Just in case.'

'Okay. But please be careful. And stay in touch.'

'Will do. Bye.'

It was after eleven, but the city streets were still busy and the night warm. Shack took a short cut through Jubilee Gardens and past the London Eye. Then along Riverside Walk, and north over Hungerford Bridge. Twenty minutes after leaving the *Belvedere,* he passed across Leicester Square. A few minutes later he was in Soho.

The tail had been using the crowds as cover. Criss-crossing the road and moving in and out of the groups of tourists. He was good, but Shack had spotted Detective Chief Inspector Stephen Bowen, well before Leicester Square.

In Soho, Shack saw the reflection of the blue flashing lights at the top end of Frith Street. When he got to the corner, he could see a crowd had gathered. An ambulance and two police cars were at the end of the service road behind *Idols*. He quickly negotiated the crowd and managed to get to the scene.

The medical crew were loading a trolley into the back of the ambulance. 'What happened?' he said to a lady bystander.

The woman pointed to a doorway, a few yards in from the end of the road. 'Some homeless person has been stabbed in there. Looks like the medics couldn't save him.'

Shack didn't reply. As he eased his way out of the crowd, he said quietly. 'I'm sorry, Chalky. God bless.'

* * *

It was almost eight o'clock the next morning, when Shack got back to Amanda's. He tapped-in the access code and went in. She was asleep on the couch when he entered. He closed the door as quietly as he could, but the click still woke her. She jumped up, rushed over and hugged him. 'Oh, I was so worried.'

He smiled. 'Hey, I'm okay, Y'Ladyship. Have you been up all night?'

She stepped back. 'Yes. I was awake most of the night after you messaged me. Must have dozed off after it got light. You're okay?'

'I'm fine, love, really. But I'm choking for a cuppa.'

'Yes of course, I'll put the kettle on. You hungry?'

He shook his head and followed her into the kitchen.

'So, what happened last night, Shack?'

As he sipped his tea, he went over the evening's events. From the lodge meeting, to being followed by Bowen and the stabbing of Chalky White. 'I got him killed.'

'What?'

'Chalky. I got him killed. If I hadn't been talking to him . . .'

'Stop it! You didn't kill him. It's a tragic event that happens in London a lot. This bloody Mayor has lost control of the city.'

He grinned at her passionate outburst.

'His death is probably not related to our investigation at all. So just stop it.'

He finished his tea. 'You may be right. But we've just lost an important witness.'

She went into the drawing room and returned with her phone. 'Not really.' She tapped the screen a couple of times, then put the device on the counter.

You stay around here? You in this street regular? . . . Why who wants to know? . . . I want to know. D'you stay

102

*around here? It's not a problem. You're not in any bother
. . . Well There's a doorway with a vent that's pretty warm.*
She switched off the phone.
'You recorded the conversation!'
She nodded. 'What can I tell you? I'm a journalist.'

* * *

In another kitchen, in North London, Detective Inspector
Stephen Bowen listened to the rant. He held the phone
away from his ear as the abuse poured out.

Finally, he spoke. 'Yes sir. I'm sorry. I was with him
until Soho, then I lost him. I'm sorry, sir I . . . No sir . . .
Yes of course . . . I'll . . .'

The phone went silent.

Linda Bowen looked at her husband. 'What was that
all about?'

He shook his head and threw the phone onto the
counter. 'A case we're working on.'

'Are you okay, Steve?'

'No, I'm bloody not okay. Now get my breakfast
ready, for Christ sake.'

Chapter Twenty Seven
'Plod'

Ruby Brennan had spent the morning at the Trafford Centre. It was almost one o'clock when she got home and pulled into her parking space. She collected her bags, locked the car, then got into the lift. On the ground floor she went to the concierge desk.

She smiled at the old guy. 'Anything for me?'

'Afternoon, Miss Brennan. Just a second.' He came back from the inner office with a couple of envelopes and a magazine. The old boy smiled. 'That's it.'

'Okay, thank you.'

As she went towards the lift, he said. 'Oh, there were two men here to see you earlier.'

She turned. 'Two men? Did they say who they were? What they wanted?'

The guy shook his head. 'Didn't say. Just wanted to see you.'

'And they never said who they were?'

He shook his head again. 'Nope . . . But I reckon they were *Five-O*.'

She frowned. 'Police? What makes you think that?'

He winked. 'When you've lived as long as I have, Miss, you can spot the plod anywhere.'

She smiled. 'Right. Thank you.'

'You're welcome, Miss.'

In her apartment, Ruby emptied the bags and hung up her new clothes. She went into the lounge and looked out the window. For several seconds she stared at the clouds, then picked up her phone and tapped the screen.

It was answered after the second beep. 'Hey, gorgeous. You okay?'

'Shack. Hi, baby. Yes, I'm fine.'

'What's up?'

'The cops have been here again. At least I think it was the police.'

'What do you mean, you think?'

'I didn't actually see them. The guy on the desk said there were two men looking for me.'

'And they said they were police?'

'No. But the old boy reckons they were plod, as he so eloquently put it.' The line was silent for several seconds. 'Shack?'

'Yeah, I'm here. Look, I think you need to get out of Manchester for a few days.'

'Get out? Why? What's going on?'

'Listen, do you trust me, darlin'?'

She grinned. 'More than anyone I know actually.'

'Okay. Then please do as I ask. Get a cab to Piccadilly and the next train to London.' Again, the line was silent, 'Ruby?'

'All right. I will. Might be nice to have a few days away.'

'Good. Message me and I'll meet you at Euston.'

'Okay, baby. Bye.'

'And, Ruby. Just be careful, eh?'

He smiled at the sound of her kisses, then hung up.

'What's happening?' said Amanda.

'Looks like the police still want to talk to Ruby. I've told her to come here. Is that okay?'

'Of course. When does she arrive?'
'She'll be down on the next rattler.'

Ruby's train got into Euston over twenty minutes late, at 18:40. Amanda and Shack were waiting at the gate as she came up the platform ramp. She eased her way through the crowd, then beamed when she saw Shack. Amanda watched as the pair hugged.

'Ruby, this is Amanda. Amanda, this is Ruby.'

The women smiled and shook hands. 'Good to meet you,' said Amanda. 'I've heard a lot about you.'

Ruby continued to smile. 'Really?' She looked over Amanda's shoulder at Shack. 'Whereas I've heard nothing about you, darling.'

Shack quickly took hold of the wheelie and said. 'Err, yes, well. Let's just get outta here, shall we, ladies?'

Chapter Twenty Eight
'Don't Mess With Me'

It was almost nine o'clock by the time Shack and the ladies had finished dinner. Yet another meal had been order-in. This time from a little Thai place a couple of blocks away. It wasn't Shack's first choice but, as the girls out-voted him, he went along with it. His meal was all the more palatable, washed down with four bottles of Budweiser.

During dinner, Shack and Amanda had explained the situation and their plans to seek justice, or revenge, for the deaths of their partners. None of which seemed to surprise or faze Ruby. Indeed, she was now keen to do all she could to help in any way possible. A fact she made eminently clear, after Shack said he'd rather she didn't become further involved.

She stood up and put her hands on her hips. The don't-mess-with-me stance, was not lost on him.

'Not get involved? The police have been after me twice. So, if you think I'm going to sit around here and do nothing you are very wrong, Mr Shackleton Blister.'

Shack got up, his face stern, then laughed out loud. He hugged her, and said, 'Whatever you say, doll.'

Amanda raised her glass to Ruby. 'Well said, girlfriend.'

The girls laughed.

'Right,' said Shack. 'I guess I know where I stand. I'll clear up.'

Amanda picked up the bottle of Pino. 'And we'll take this out onto the balcony.'

Outside, Ruby said, 'This is a lovely location.'

'Yes. We were lucky to get it. Sam and I were really happy here.'

'I'm sure. And I'm sorry, darling.'

Amanda topped up Ruby's glass. For a while they sat in silence. The riverside lights, and those of Hammersmith Bridge, were reflected in the dark waters of the Thames.

'So, how long have you known Shack?' said Amanda.

'It'll be over two years now. Pretty much since he came out of prison.'

'Ah, okay. And how did you actually meet?'

Ruby smiled, then drank some wine. 'It was late, almost midnight. I'd been to see a client at the *Midland Hotel*. I was outside on the steps, waiting for my cab. There were still a few people about. Across the road from the hotel, there was a bit of a scuffle going on. Three young lads having a go at a drunk, pushing him about, taunting him. Anyway, I watched for a minute or two, then the drunk lashed out and knocked one down. It turned nasty and they set about him. He had no chance. I shouted across. The doorman came out and I told him to go sort them out. He said to stay out of it. They were really laying into the guy now. I ran across the road and shouted at them. They turned and laughed at me, then carried on kicking the guy. I pulled one off. Sprayed Mace at another. His screams really shook the other two up. I was waving the Mace about . . . then they decided to take off.'

'My God, Ruby! Then what happened?'

'The guy was moaning. His face bleeding. I saw he only had one eye. I called an ambulance, went to the hospital with him, made sure he was okay, and then went home.'

'Did he know you helped him?'

'Not at the time. They wanted my name at the hospital. I guess once he was compos mentis they told him. A couple of days later he showed up at my flat.'

'Really?'

'Yes. With a lovely bouquet of flowers. He was still pretty battered and bruised, but sober.'

'And?'

'We chatted for a while. We went out for lunch the next day. Had a dinner date a few days later and a lovely night together. He was so gentle, so sweet. I saw him a couple more times. Then told him I was an escort.'

'What did he say to that?'

'Not much . . . that I should be careful. Seemed genuinely concerned. Anyway, he started to see me regularly, but every time he paid me. I told him I didn't want money, that he was my friend, that I cared for him. He still gives me money now. The idiot. Sometimes we just go out for a meal. Or a movie. He's good company when he's not too drunk.'

Amanda laughed.

'I never used anything he gave me. Put it in an ISA, in his name. One of these days I might be able to give it back to him. The stubborn sod.'

'And you've been friends ever since.'

Ruby took a deep breath. 'He's a great guy. Kind, gentle and very funny when he wants to be. He got me into the property business, you know. He had a client who was involved with repossessions. Shack would give me the heads up and I'd pick them up at a good price. I have a nice little portfolio now.'

The girls sipped at their wine, then Amanda said, 'Do you love him, Ruby?'

'Wow . . . That was direct, darling.'

Amanda grinned. 'Well?'

Ruby took a drink of wine, then smiled. 'Yes . . . I guess so.'

Chapter Twenty Nine
'Hello Maria'

Shack had spent a fitful night struggling with the haunting nightmare of the crash. He was shaken awake, a little after sunrise, by Amanda and Ruby.

'What the hell . . . What's happening?' he shouted.

Ruby and Amanda stood at the bedside. 'You were screaming,' said Amanda.

He sat up. 'Aww shit. I'm sorry.'

'Are you okay?' asked Ruby. 'You're covered in sweat.'

'Yeah, I'm fine. Bloody nightmares. What time is it?'

'Almost five o'clock,' said Amanda.

'Oh, I'm sorry, ladies. Go back to bed. I'm okay now. I'll get up and shower.'

'You sure?' said Ruby. 'You want me to stay with you?'

'No. I'm fine. Really. I'm fine.' He grinned. 'Probably just that awful Thai food we had.'

After they left his room, Amanda turned to Ruby. 'Thai food?'

Ruby frowned and shook her head. 'No. I've seen that before. It's the accident.'

It was almost eight o'clock when Amanda came out onto the balcony. Shack was there reading the paper. She put a hand on his shoulder. 'Good morning. Feeling better, partner?'

With a sheepish grin he, said, 'Yeah, sorry about earlier. Is Ruby awake?'

'Don't think so. Didn't hear anything from her room. You want some breakfast?'

He shook his head. 'No thanks, love.'

'Tea?'

He smiled and nodded.

* * *

In Manchester, the café on Salford's North Quay was busy with the breakfast regulars. Two men sat down.

Maria smiled as she approached. 'Good morning gentlemen. What can I get you?'

The older guy answered in Polish. 'Nothing, but there is someone who wants a word with you.'

'What?'

He leaned closer. 'Don't worry, we are not going to hurt you.' He stood up and pointed to the big Mercedes. 'The car's just there.'

The younger man took hold of her arm. She tried to pull away. 'Let go of me.'

A couple of the other customers noticed the exchange. The man released her, then smiled. 'Okay, now?'

The rear door of the car opened, and a well-dressed woman beckoned her. Maria looked around. The café and quayside were quite busy so the chance of anything happening seemed small. She went to the car. 'What do you want with me?'

The woman smiled. She also spoke in Polish. 'Hello, Maria.'

'You know me?'

'Yes, we know you, my dear. You are Maria Krol, from Gdansk. Where your mother and father still live.' She picked up her phone and swiped the screen. Turning it to Maria, she said, 'They look so happy.'

Maria looked at the photo of her parents. 'What do you want?'

'Don't worry we aren't going to harm them. Unless of course . . . Well . . . just get in.'

Maria shook her head.

'If we wanted to hurt you it would be very easy for us to do so.'

'I'm supposed to be working.'

'This will only take a minute. Get in, please.'

'Leave the door open and I will.'

'No problem, my dear. Now get in.'

Maria slipped into the seat, one leg outside the car, ready to run. 'So?'

'Have you heard of The Red Queen, Maria?' The woman smiled at the girl's reaction.

'Yes. I have.'

'I work for The Red Queen and she may require you to do something for her.'

'I'm not . . .'

The woman raised a perfectly manicured finger. 'Just listen, please.' She opened her bag and took out an envelope. 'There's a thousand pounds in here for this few minutes of your time. I believe you have a break in an hour. Meet me over there in the parking area at ten.'

'But I . . .'

Again, the finger was raised, and the envelope dropped onto Maria's lap. The woman smiled. 'See you in an hour, my dear.'

Chapter Thirty
'Call Me Karen'

The rest of the morning was spent looking for a suitable site, to put the first part of Shack's plan into action. They were back at the Hammersmith flat by 2pm. On the balcony the three sat with drinks, sparkling water for the girls and Bud for Shack. His first bottle never touched the sides. He cracked the cap on a second bottle, and said, 'Okay, let's go through it again.'

Ruby gave a deep sigh. 'Really? We've been over and over it!'

Shack frowned, his one good eye almost closed, intimidating.

Ruby laughed. 'That look won't work with me, mister.'

He shook his head. 'Okay, but please, just indulge me.'

The girls looked at each other, then simultaneously raised their eyebrows.

Fifteen minutes later, he said, 'Okay, that's it. Anyone want a sandwich? I'm starving.'

* * *

The building, a small office complex in Battersea, was almost finished. Construction work was complete and final-fix looked to be underway, with several areas already decorated. The site had been secured, but Shack had cut off the original lock and swapped it for a new one.

Ruby had the key and waited in the rented Audi. She adjusted the red wig and put on the oversized sunglasses.

Donny Black pulled-up a little after 6pm. He parked next to her and got out. She stepped out and offered her hand. As they shook, he said, 'Sorry I'm late, Miss Anders, damn traffic.'

Ruby smiled. 'Call me Karen. Let's go in.'

'So, when are your offices due to open, Karen?'

She unfastened the big padlock, and said, 'We're behind schedule, which is a problem. So, we really need your security quote as soon as possible.'

He grinned. 'That's what I'm here for.'

They stepped through the temporary hoarding and into the site, then used the lock to secure the door. 'Let's start over here.'

The office space was still crowded with materials, mostly large bales of insulation. Black looked around, then began making notes on his pad. 'Okay, Karen. We can do a . . .'

'Don't move Donny!' said Shack, as he prodded him in the back. 'This shooter's got a hair trigger.'

'What the fuck?'

'I said don't move!' The pressure against Donny's back increased. 'This will rip your kidney out.'

'Bobby?'

Shack leaned forward and looked over Black's shoulder. 'Yeah. It's me.'

'What the hell's going on?'

'We need a little chat with you, me old mate. Put your hands behind your back.'

The security man was fit and fast. He took half a step to the side and spun on his heels, knocking the piece of copper pipe from Shack's hand. It fell to the floor with a metallic clatter. The pain in Shack's chest, as Donny elbowed him, was unbelievable. Shack gasped for breath, but still managed an uppercut, hitting Black on the chin. The bigger man staggered back, but soon recovered and lunged. The vicious headbutt split Shack's nose across the bridge. Donny raised a huge fist, to finish him off. Ruby rushed forward with her telescopic police baton. But it was the crack of the gunshot that stopped Donny in his tracks.

Amanda appeared from behind the bales. 'That's enough!' Her gun pointed directly at Donny Black. A fine wisp of blue smoke floated from the muzzle, as the rank smell of cordite filled the air.

* * *

Back in Amanda's kitchen, she watched Ruby clean and dress the gash on Shack's nose. 'I think you're going to have a black eye as well, baby,' said Ruby.

Shack took a swallow of malt and grinned. 'I'll just put the patch over it.'

Ruby shook her head. 'Idiot.' She planted a gentle kiss on the end of his nose and stepped back. 'Okay, there you go.'

Shack finished off the whisky, then poured another. He turned to Amanda. 'A gun? You have a gun?'

'Yes.'

'Why didn't you say?'

'Because I knew you wouldn't use it.'

'You're bloody right I wouldn't.'

'Well, it's just as well I took it. Your bit of pipe idea didn't work, did it?'

'It was only till we had him tied up.'

'Right. Well we saw how that turned out.' She took a glass from the cupboard and poured herself a very large malt.

'Whoa, Y'Ladyship. Take it easy with that stuff.'

She swallowed a mouthful, then coughed as the strong liquid hit the back of her throat.

'You okay?' said Ruby.

Amanda coughed again. 'Yes. I'm fine.' She took another glass and filled it from the tap. She sipped some water. 'I was concerned . . . Okay?'

Shack stood up and hugged her. 'Hey, you did right, all things considered. So, thank you.'

She smiled and hugged him back.

Shack sat down again. He frowned. 'So, where the hell did you get a shooter?'

In an overly posh accent, she said, 'We're landed gentry, darling. Hunting, shooting, fishing is all we really know how to do.'

Shack and Ruby laughed. 'But where did you get it?' said Shack.

Amanda turned and left the kitchen. A few moments later she returned and handed him a sheet of paper. Shack rubbed his eye, then looked at the document. At the top of the page was an embossed image of a portcullis, beneath was written, The Home Office.

Intrigued, Ruby said, 'What is it?'

Shack glanced at her, then began reading . . . *This document approves and grants the bearer the use of firearms, in Defence of the Realm, and with my full consent* . . . He placed the letter on the counter, then looked at Amanda. 'You have authorisation from the Home Secretary!'

Amanda took a deep breath and picked up the paper. As she slowly folded it she said, 'Samantha . . . Samantha was given this along with the Walther, the gun. And yes, the Home Secretary approved it. When she came home with it I was shocked. But Sam said she'd no intention of carrying it.' Amanda picked up her glass and took another sip of whisky. 'Now I wish she had. She might still be alive today.'

Shack stood up and hugged her again. 'Hey, it's okay, love. It's okay.

She smiled, then finished off her malt.

Shack leaned forward and put his elbows on the counter. He looked at the women for several seconds. 'You've got a gun and you've got Mace and a riot baton.' He shook his head. 'You girls are turning into the wild bunch.'

Chapter Thirty One
'The Weakest Link'

The following morning, Lena Stavos listened as the man on the phone spoke. She made little comment other than a few, 'Okay's.' The phone call over, she left the stables and went out to the exercise ring. A magnificent new stallion had just arrived from the continent and one of the boys was giving it a run round. She watched the animal for several minutes then took out her phone. She swiped the screen and waited.

After half a dozen rings the call was answered by Lord Edward Valentine. 'Lena, hello! What a lovely surprise.'

'Hello, Edward. Sorry to disturb you, but might you have time to meet?'

'I'm always happy to be disturbed by you, my dear. And I can certainly find time to meet,' gushed Valentine. 'When?'

'As soon as possible really. I thought we could have a quiet dinner and then, perhaps rather than drive back to the city, you could stay over?'

'That's sounds wonderful. There's a vote tonight, so I really should be in the House, but I can miss that and be there about eight-ish?'

'Perfect. I'll have chef prepare that Sea Bream you enjoy so much.'

'My mouth is watering all ready.'

'Good. Until this evening then. Bye, Edward.'

'Cheerio, my dear.'

In the Hammersmith flat, Shack and the girls were on the balcony, discussing the previous evening's encounter with Donny Black.

'You think he'll go for it?' said Ruby.

Shack adjusted the eyepatch, then took a deep breath. *'The most robust chain is only as strong as its weakest link. Strive to exploit your enemies weakest link.'*

Ruby frowned. 'Really? You're quoting, Sun Tzu's Art of War?'

Shack grinned. 'Yeah.'

'And you still think the sleezy Mr Black, is the weakest link?' said Amanda.

'I do. And as long as he believes we have the evidence to put him away for the three C's, we have him by the balls. If you'll pardon the expression, ladies.'

'The three C's?' said Ruby

Shack nodded. 'The three C's. Collusion, conspiracy and corruption,'

Amanda smiled. 'I actually think it might just work. That, or the police will be breaking down my front door in the not too distant future.'

'So, when do we move to phase two, boss?' said Ruby.

'Soon, babe. Soon.'

* * *

Lord Valentine's day seemed to drag on forever. He was keen to get out of the city and on his way to Lena's as soon as possible. He finally arrived at The Red Queen's Buckinghamshire estate a few minutes before 8pm and, as always, was excited at the prospect of a night with the exotic Lena. Drinks on the patio overlooking the lake, were followed by a delicious meal in the dining room. Staff dismissed; they withdrew to the sitting room with a second bottle of Crystal. Small talk ensued until sun set, a little after ten-thirty, when an excellent Armagnac was taken up to Lena's bedroom as a night-cap.

She enjoyed Valentine's company. He was intelligent and ruthless, which matched her personality perfectly. And, even though decidedly older than her usual younger lovers, he was vigorous when needed and always took time to ensure her pleasure superseded his own.

At one o'clock he excused himself and got out of bed. In the bathroom he urinated, then washed his hands. He looked at his reflection in the mirror, then ran his fingers through the thick mop of grey hair. He smiled and said quietly, 'You old dog, you.'

As he came back into the room, she said, 'Are you okay, darling?'

'Wonderful, my dear. Just wonderful.'

She sat up in bed, her youthful breasts still glistened with perspiration. 'I need to talk to you, Edward.' She patted the bed next to her. 'Come here.'

He frowned. 'Of course, my dear. Is something wrong?'

'Yes. I'm afraid so.'

Chapter Thirty Two
'Sofia'

Following an urgent call from his office, Valentine had declined breakfast. He'd left at seven-fifteen, waved-off from her bedroom balcony by the lovely Lena. Even before his Bentley had passed through the main gates, she was on the phone.

The Turzo brothers had worked for the Stavos organisation ever since their arrival in the UK, six years ago. Not identical twins and with fifteen minutes difference in age, Milosh and Leon were not only brothers, they were best friends. At thirty two years old, a more charming and presentable pair one could not wish to meet. Dressed in designer suits and Breitling watches, they looked more like stockbrokers than assassins and were the tip-of-the-spear when it came to dispatching punishment or death, on behalf of The Red Queen.

Following her early morning call, the brothers had left their south London apartment and immediately headed out to Ealing. The drive had taken longer than expected, due to some kind of terrorist incident in the city. The rush-hour, compounded by several diversions, caused chaos throughout the capital and made them almost an hour late getting to *The Larches* public house.

Situated on the edge of town the old pub, with its walls covered in dozens of photos of famous stars, was still one of the main watering holes for today's lesser known actors and crews from the nearby film studios.

Their contact had finished shooting her scenes over three hours ago and now awaited the Turzo's arrival. She was with a small group of extras, having a late breakfast, when Milosh and Leon entered. She excused herself and went out to the rear beer garden. The Turzo twins followed.

'Good to see you again, Sofia,' said Leon. He pointed to her hand. 'What happened?'

'Yeah, nice to see you too. This?' She held up the heavily bandaged appendage. 'Bloody gag went wrong. Got my hand got caught in the car door as I jumped.'

Milosh frowned. 'I thought you were one of the best stunt-women in the business?'

'Yes, well. We all have off-days. You guys want some brunch? A drink?'

Leon shook his head. 'No thanks, we need to get back to the city. We've something on later.'

'How's your mother?' said Leon.

'She's fine, thank you. Coming over from Poland for a holiday soon.'

The Turzos smiled and nodded in unison.

'Okay, boys. To business. What can I do for you?'

Milosh passed her a large brown envelope. 'Target. Address. Car. Movements. There's a truck in there for you as well. The Queen wants this doing as soon as possible. Top priority.'

She put the envelope in her bag. 'Okay. I'm off for a couple of days,' she raised her hand, 'thanks to this. I can get right on it.'

Milosh nodded. 'Good.'

'And my fee?'

Another smaller envelope was passed across the table. 'Half now, half after.'

She smiled and slipped the second envelope into her bag. 'Right. I'd better get organised.' She stood up and kissed each of the twins. 'One of these days we really should get together, boys.' She winked, then headed back into the pub.

As they watched her walk away, Milosh said, 'I would.'

Leon smirked. 'So would I.'

* * *

Detective Inspector Stephen Bowen's day had been bad. The early morning terrorist incident had every security agency in the city working flat out. He'd managed to wangle an hour off, to go home for a shower and let his wife know he'd be working all night.

His north London home, in the pleasant suburb of Stamford Hill, was a far cry from the frantic hustle and bustle of the city. As he drove off the busy A10, onto Lynmouth Road, he breathed a deep sigh. He was only a couple of hundred yards from his house when he saw the builder's truck coming towards him.

He flashed his light and pressed hard on the horn. The truck kept coming.

'Shit!' He threw the car into reverse, but ground the gears almost stalling his vehicle.

The truck accelerated, looming ever bigger in the windscreen.

'What the fuck!' he yelled.

He swung the wheel side to side, as he reversed away from the oncoming truck. In his panic he smashed into one of the cars parked along the side of the road, stopping him dead . . .

'Nooooo . . .'

The thunderous sound of the crash brought a dozen or so residents rushing from their homes. The gruesome scene caused one young woman to vomit; another screamed. Several people were on their phones. A pair of teenagers stood and videoed the macabre tableaux.

The tangle of steel and glass was horrific. The builder's truck had ploughed over the bonnet and smashed into the interior with devastating force, leaving Bowen's decapitated body crushed below its big heavy axle.

A hundred yards away Sofia Novak turned the corner, her breathing relaxed and steady, as she jogged towards Stamford Hill tube station. She quickly removed her black jacket and turned it inside out, then slipped it back on. The black woollen hat concealing her hair was removed and stuffed into her pocket, letting her hair fall free. Her gloves and big sunglass went into the other pocket just as she arrived at the station.

As she passed through the barrier she smiled at the ticket attendant. He returned the smile and watched as the nice blonde lady in a red jacket made her way to the platform.

Chapter Thirty Three
'Local News'

Deputy Commander Thomas Morrison's day had also been challenging. There'd been a follow-up terrorist incident and several response meetings would be going on late into the night.

The strange hit-and-run crash and subsequent death of Detective Inspector Stephen Bowen was being broadcast on the local ten o'clock news. Morrison watched the report.

One eyewitness said, 'It was strange, it seemed as if the truck was out of control, as if the driver was unable to stop. It just kept on going. It was awful.'

Another said, 'Yeah, I saw the driver. He wore black pants, jacket and hat. He jumped out and ran off up the street. Didn't give a toss for the poor sod he'd ploughed into. Must've been drunk or on drugs or something.'

Morrison struggled to keep the shocked looked from his face. He excused himself from the meeting and went out onto the street.

His call was answered almost immediately. 'Was that crash anything to do with us?'

Sir Anthony Fairfax didn't speak. Several moments passed.

'Sir Anthony?'

'Yes, Tom, I'm here. And to what crash do you refer?'

'Bowen. Stephen Bowen. That crash. He's dead. Or didn't you know?'

'Yes, I know, Tom.'

'Was that an accident or something else?'

'Something else?'

'Yes, something else. And if it was, why the fuck was I not advised first?'

'Calm down, Tom. I do not take kindly to your tone.'

'My tone? Jesus, I . . .'

'Stop right there, Commander. Firstly, we should not be discussing this issue on the telephone. And secondly, you work for us, not the other way round.'

Two police cars, sirens screaming; lights flashing; roared down the street.

Morrison waited, then said, 'That's as may be, but Bowen operated under me. So again, I ask, why was I not advised?'

'Information had come to light which may impact on us all, Tom. So, our friend in Buckinghamshire arranged to have the problem taken care of.'

'Information? What information? And from whom?'

'I'm hanging up Tom. We cannot continue on the phone.'

'Just a minute I . . .' the line buzzed. 'Hello? Hello? . . . Bastard!'

* * *

In Hammersmith, Shack was going for more drinks. He stopped in the lounge and watched the unfolding story on the late evening news. 'Jesus Christ!'

The girls came in from the balcony. 'What is it?' said Amanda.

Shack nodded towards the television. 'Look.'

'Oh, my God,' said Ruby, 'is that us? Did we cause this?'

Amanda, seeing how shocked Ruby was, put an arm around her shoulders. 'We didn't do anything, darling. This is the people we're up against.'

Shack turned from the TV. 'At the risk of sounding callous, this would suggest our little chat with Donny Black has been successful.'

Ruby stepped forward. 'Successful? We caused that man's death.'

He looked at Ruby and said nothing for several seconds, then turned and headed for the kitchen.

'Nothing to say?' snapped Ruby.

Amanda stepped forward and touched Ruby's arm. 'Leave it, darling.'

Shack stopped. 'These bastards are responsible for killing my family. These bastards are responsible for killing Samantha. You want me to feel sorry if one of them gets killed? If they start killing each other?' He slowly shook his head. 'No.' He put the empty glasses on the table, then turned and went to his room. He returned a few seconds later with his jacket on.

'What are you doing?' said Amanda.

'I'm goin' to get some air. See you guys later.'

'Shack, please, wait,' said Ruby 'I . . .'

He raised his hand. 'It's okay, love. See you later.'

As the door closed the women looked at each other and said nothing.

Chapter Thirty Four
'One For The Road'

Once outside, Shack checked his watch, ten-twenty. He looked up and down the street, then turned and headed towards the pub at the end of the next block.

The place was quite busy with locals. A three piece jazz group were squeezed onto a small stage in the corner. The music was good and the atmosphere pleasant.

He took a seat at the end of the bar. 'Pint of Stella and a large Glenfiddich, please.' By closing time at eleven-thirty, he'd downed another four rounds of the same. He straightened the eye patch and grinned at the barman. 'One more for the road, mate.'

The man shook his head. 'You've had enough, sir and it's gone last orders. Sorry.'

Shack mumbled something as he rose from the stool. Outside a couple of blackcabs stood waiting for punters. He climbed into the back of the lead taxi.

'Where to, boss?'

'Soho, mate. *Idols.*'

Fifteen minutes later Shack woke to the sound of the driver's voice. 'Sir . . . Sir . . . We're here . . . Sir.'

'Okay, okay. How much?'

'Twelve quid, sir.'

Shack pushed fifteen pounds through the slot in the screen. 'Cheers, mate. Keep the change.'

The usual Saturday night queue was building outside *Idols.* Shack disregarded the chants of 'Get to the back!'

from several of the impatient patrons in the line. One of the burly doormen shook his head as Shack approached. 'Yes, sir?'

'What?' said Shack.

'Can I help you?'

'No thanks, mate Just gonna have a nightcap.'

'Not in here, sir. Sorry, I think you've had enough.'

'Bollocks, I 'ave.'

'Okay, pal, move along.'

'Donny!'

'What?'

'Donny Black. I need to speak with him.'

'Not tonight. Now move along.'

'Get on your bloody headphone and tell him Shack . . . Bobby Stone, is here.'

The bouncer turned and spoke into his head-mic. A couple of seconds later he turned back and stood to one side. 'Okay, sir. In you go.'

Another shout of, 'Oh, come on! We've been here for ages,' came from the queue.

The club was packed, the noise seemed louder than usual, thanks to what looked like several hen parties screaming and singing. It took a few moments for Shack to locate Donny at the bar. As he made his way over he stumbled on the steps up to the counter.

'Jesus, your pissed,' said Black.

Shack recovered his balance and joined him at the counter. 'Nah. Not yet. I'm still standing.'

'What the hell do you want, Bobby?'

'I'll have a large malt. Cheers, mate.'

'I didn't mean a drink. What do you want?'

Shack grinned. 'Okay. Just a beer, then.'

Black nodded to the Madonna lookalike behind the bar. A few seconds later a bottle of Bud was placed in front of Shack.

'Cheers, Donny,' he said, then swallowed half the contents of the bottle.

'So, what're you doing here?'

'I want a word with you me, ol' mate. But I can't hear bugger all in here.'

'Okay. Come on.'

Shack followed him through the crowd and out of the main club, through a door marked FIRE EXIT and out into the rear corridor.

'Better?' said Black.

'Yeah. Much.'

'So?'

'Detective Inspector Stephen Bowen.' He finished off the beer and put the empty bottle on floor, almost losing his balance as he did so. 'Ooops,' he said as he straightened up.

Donny smirked at the drunk before him. 'What about him?'

'Did our little agreement have anything to do with his death?'

Black frowned. 'What?'

'Was our deal the cause of Bowen's death? Was he killed because of . . .'

'No.'

Shack leaned unsteadily against the wall. 'What?'

Donny stepped a little closer, he frowned again at the strong smell of whisky. 'Bowen had taken to working for himself. He was ripping off the Red Queen. She had him taken out. Was nothing to do with our deal.'

'You sure?'

'Yes, I'm fucking sure. Now is there anything else you want to know?'

Shack, a stupid grin on his face said, 'Nah . . . That's it me, ol' mate.'

Another bouncer entered the corridor. 'Everything all right, boss?'

Donny stepped away from Shack. 'Yeah. All okay, Steve. This gentlemen was just leaving. You can help him out the back door.'

'Aw, not one for the road then, Donny?'

The bouncer took hold of Shack and began moving him to the rear door. 'Err, Steve,' said Black.'

'Yes, boss?'

'Give him a good slap as well.'

In the back street the bouncer looked at the hapless drunk and shook his head. In doorman's terms 'a good slap' could mean anything from a headbutt, to a good kicking. Neither of which Steve intended to do. But as his boss may well have be watching from the security monitors, he carried out his orders and gave the one-eyed man a good punch in the stomach.

The blow knocked the breath from Shack's body. He let out a loud groan, 'Ahhh!' then proceeded to throw up most of the night's alcohol.

'Christ,' said Steve, as he quickly stepped back from the vomiting man; then watched as he fell to the floor and pass out. He thought of putting the boot in but turned and went back inside the club.

A few seconds later a shadow fell across the motionless figure. Tina Turner's punch line, from the movie 'Thunderdome' was lost on the unconscious Shack. 'Well, well, well, Raggedy Man . . . ain't we a pair.'

Chapter Thirty Five
'Come Back, Love'

The sun streamed in through the open window and the cool Sunday morning breeze freshened the air.

Semiconscious, Shack saw Chrissy bent over him. Gently shaking his shoulder. 'Come on. Come on. Wake up.'

Shack groaned and slowly stirred. The sudden slap on his face brought him to his senses 'What the hell!'

'Come on, mate, wake up.'

He opened his eye. Chrissy was gone. Replaced by a man's face leaning over him. 'What the . . .?' He swung his legs off the couch and sat up. 'Where am I?'

'You're in my gaff, mate. You were in a right state last night.'

Shack looked at the man for several seconds, then realisation dawned. 'Chalky?'

The man grinned. 'The very same.'

'I thought you were dead . . . in the alley . . . the ambulance.'

'No, mate, not me. That was some other poor sod.'

Shack looked around the room. Clean, tidy, comfortable. Nice furniture. Big-screen TV. The smell of fresh coffee. 'So, this is your place?'

'Yeah. You want some coffee?'

Shack shook his head. 'Water then, tea. If that's okay? And I need the toilet.'

'No probs, mate. Bathroom is through there. Oh, and there's a new toothbrush in the cabinet. I suggest you use it. Your breath's like a badger's arse.' Chalky turned and went into the kitchen.

Shack got up and went to the bathroom. A few minutes later he entered the kitchen. 'I don't get it,' he said.

Chalky filled a glass with tap water and passed it across. 'Get what?'

'This place. You. I thought you were . . .'

'Homeless?'

Shack swallowed the water. 'Yeah, homeless. Or is that just a con?'

Chalky frowned. 'No con, mate. It's a long story.'

'I'm all ears, but I need to make a call first.' He took his phone out. 'Shit!'

'What?'

'Smashed screen and the battery's out.'

'Give it here.' Chalky took it, then removed his own phone from its charger cable. He plugged in Shack's and said, 'There you go. It's powering-up, so it should work.'

Shack nodded. 'Cheers.'

The call was answered on the second ring. 'Shack! Are you all right?'

'Yeah, I'm fine, Y'Ladyship.'

'Thank God. Where are you?'

'Err, not really sure. But I'm okay. I'll be back soon. Can I have a quick word with Ruby, please?'

'She's gone, Shack.'

'Gone? Gone where. Not Manchester?'

'No. She left a couple of hours ago. Took the hire-car and said she was going to stay with her parents in Leeds, until things calmed down. She must be halfway up the M1 by now.'

135

'Right, thanks, love. I'll see if I can get her. Will be back soon.'

'Okay. Take care.'

The line went dead. Chalky said, 'Here's your tea, mate.'

Shack swallowed a mouthful, then tapped the cracked screen. It took a few rings until the call was answered. 'Hello?'

'Ruby. Hi, gorgeous.'

'Hey, baby. How are you? You okay?'

'Yeah. Long story, but I'm fine. Where are you? What're you doing?'

'I've just stopped at a service area near Leicester. I'm going to my parents.'

'Listen, love, come back, there's no need to leave.'

'I'm sorry, Shack, but I can't be responsible for anyone getting killed. I . . .'

'You're not. We're not. Bowen's death had nothing to do with us, or Black.'

'What do you mean?'

'I promise you, Ruby, nothing we've done had anything to do with Bowen. Come back and I'll explain the whole story.'

'Really?'

'Really. Turn around and get back here. Please, love.'

The line was silent for a few seconds, and then. 'Okay. I'll see you in a couple of hours.'

'Great. See you soon. Drive safely, gorgeous.'

The line went dead. Shack picked up the mug and finished his tea.

'You got a few ladies on the go there, Mr Blister.'

'Call me Shack. And it's not what it looks like.'

Chalky winked. 'Yeah, right.'

Shack made a sweeping gesture with his hand., 'So, you gonna tell me what all this is about?'

Chalky nodded. 'Sure. But I'd like to know what you're up to first?'

'How do you mean?'

'Twice I've met you and both times at the back of *Idols*. A woman is killed, and you show up asking about her. A few days later you get bounced out of the same joint. The business card you gave me says you're a private detective in Manchester. So, what are you doing in London?'

Shack frowned. 'Right, good question. So, we both have a story to tell. You're not homeless and you're not running a con. I'm guessing you're a cop undercover. Right?'

'Not a cop either, mate. Let's go sit down and tell each other tall tales. You never know, we might even be on the same side.'

'The same side of what?'

Chalky grinned. 'That's what we need to find out.'

* * *

Shack left Chalky's flat just after eleven. He took the tube from Paddington and arrived at Hammersmith twenty-five minutes later. He walked down to the Thames and set off towards Amanda's apartment. Friendly dog-walkers and joggers nodded or said. 'Good morning,' as they passed by.

As he strolled along the walkway, his thoughts were filled with the discussion he'd had with Chalky White. He stopped and looked across the water at a pair of guys racing each other in skulls. A dog on an extending lead sniffed merrily at his feet. He looked down, then smiled when its owner said, 'Sorry.'

The walk seemed to clear his head and he got back to Amanda's a few minutes before midday. As he went up in the lift his phone beeped an incoming text. He swiped the cracked screen and read Ruby's message *Stuck on M1 south of Luton.* He replied, *OK Drive safe x*

A few moments later he entered the apartment. 'Morning, Y'Ladyship,' he said sheepishly.

She shook her head, then hugged him. 'You bugger! Why didn't you call? I was so worried.' Her nose wrinkled. 'Oh, and you smell awful.'

He stepped back. 'Let me get a shower. Then I'll fill you in.'

'Okay, good. D'you want something to eat? Some tea?'

'No thanks, love. Could murder a beer though.'

She frowned. 'I'll make some tea.'

After he'd showered and changed, they sat out on the balcony with, much to his disappointment, a pot of tea. It took the best part of an hour to go through the previous night's events. The meeting with Donny Black; the revelation that Chalky White was not dead; and his subsequent help. The most amazing part of the story though, was what Chalky was actually involved in.

At one-forty-five the door opened, and Ruby came in. Shack stood up and smiled. She dashed across and hugged him. 'I'm sorry about last night. I'm sorry what I said. I think it was shock more than anything else.'

He gently took her face in his hands and smiled. 'I know, baby. It's okay. Really.'

Amanda came in from the balcony and saw the tender scene. 'Oh sorry!'

The embrace over, Shack said, 'It's fine. We were just clearing the air.'

Amanda smiled. 'Good,' she looked at Ruby, 'can I get you anything, darling? Coffee?'

'Oh, yes, please.'

Shack went to the kitchen door. 'I'll make it.'

As he disappeared inside, Amanda hugged Ruby. 'Good to have you back. You two okay now?'

Ruby nodded. 'We're okay.'

Chapter Thirty Six
'Never Trust Anyone Who Doesn't Steal'

The *Tideway* is a section of the Thames, downstream from Teddington Lock. This area of river, as the name suggests, is a tidal stretch of waterway that recedes twice a day. At low-tide the smelly, and decidedly unpleasant, silted riverbed is exposed.

It was a little after 3pm when the young detective constable arrived at the riverside location. He walked down the short flight of steps and stopped. The crime scene was about thirty feet from where he stood. 'Aw shit. This is all I need on a Sunday afternoon.'

As he stepped out onto the riverbed his feet sank into the filthy mud, engulfing his shiny shoes. The sucking noise, as he made his way to the bodies, sounded alien. The mud got deeper the further out he walked and splashed onto the bottom of his trousers.

The older police sergeant looked at him as he approached, then down at the young detectives mud-caked feet and pants. He grinned and shook his head. 'You're always gonna need boots when you get a river-shout, son.'

The detective frowned. 'Yes. Well, maybe next time eh? So, what do we have, Sergeant?'

The cop nodded towards the ground. 'As you see, we have two bodies. Scenes of Crime are on their way, but it looks pretty obvious what killed them.' The sergeant pointed to the heads. 'Looks like their skulls have been cleaved open. Machete or a heavy axe, I reckon.'

The detective turned away and vomited.

'Jesus, you'd better move away, son. SOCO won't be happy if they have to tramp through your puke as well as this mud.'

The detective took out a crumpled tissue and wiped his mouth. 'Looks like they're tied together?'

The old cop grinned. 'Yeah. Maybe they were close, eh?'

'I don't think this is a cause for levity, Sergeant.'

'Right, sorry. Anyway, whoever saw these two off certainly got their message out.'

'Message?'

'Listen, son. Sorry. Detective. This stretch of the Thames is tidal, as I'm sure you realise. And if you wanted to get rid of a body, then this is the last place you'd do it.

'Err . . . Is it?'

The old sergeant shook his head. 'Because it's gonna get washed up at some point.' He nodded to the two corpses in the mud. 'Just like these two poor buggers.'

'You said a message, Sergeant?'

'Yeah . . . the hands.'

The detective frowned. 'The hands?'

Again, the sergeant nodded to the bodies. 'They've both had their right hands chopped off. If that's not a message, I don't know what is.'

* * *

It was almost 9pm when Lena Stavos, astride the newly-arrived stallion, trotted up to the stables entrance. It was her habit to take a short evening hack around the estate and the cooler evening air seemed to calm the somewhat skittish animal. She'd become an excellent horsewoman and made a striking figure in her tight riding breeches and snug-fitting jacket. A sight that was not lost on the two leering Turzo twins.

A stable girl rushed up and took the bridle as Lena dismounted. The twins clearly enjoyed the view of Lena's behind as she did so.

Milosh leaned closer to his brother and whispered. 'I would.'

Leon grinned and whispered back, 'So would I.'

Lena turned. 'Sorry, boys. I missed that?'

'Just saying what a great looking horse, boss.'

She smiled. She could imagine what they'd said and was not unhappy that the younger members of her organisation found her desirable. 'Yes, he is rather a splendid beast.'

'Will that be all for this evening, Miss Lena?' asked the stable girl.

Lena took off her hat and gloves, then nodded. 'Yes, thank you, Anna.'

As they walked to the main house, Leon said, 'Did you see the six o'clock news, boss?'

She continued walking. 'Yes, I saw it. Nice job, boys. That'll send the right message to our people.'

The twins beamed at the Red Queen's praise. 'Cheers, boss.'

'Those two idiots and that fool, Detective Bowen, thought they could steal from us and get away with it. They were wrong.'

'Have you decided who'll replace the two idiots?' asked Milosh.

'Between them, they handled almost a hundred and eighty of our car-wash locations. That's a lot of turnover. And a great deal more with the other money we rinse through them.'

The brothers nodded in unison.

'I do have someone I'm going to use.'

'Anyone we know, boss?'

Lena stopped on the front steps. She turned and looked at the Turzos, the slightest of frowns on her face. 'You boys seem very interested in what's going on all of a sudden.'

'Err, no, no, Miss Lena,' said a worried looking Leon. 'We just . . .'

'Calm down, boys. I'm kidding.' The twins look of relief made her smile. 'Magda Wozniak, will take over those units.'

'But isn't she already running two of the casinos?'

Lena nodded. 'Yes, and without any problems. She's smart, loyal and only steals a little from us.' The brothers puzzled looks made her smile again. 'Never trust anyone who doesn't steal, boys. If they're not stealing a little, they're going to steal a lot.'

The Turzos grinned, then Leon said, 'And they end up in the Thames with their hands chopped off.'

Lena's eyes narrowed. 'Exactly.'

Chapter Thirty Seven
'Lunch Guest'

Monday morning was overcast and humid, with the threat of thunder. Donny Black was on the jogging machine and just about to finish his 45 minute run. The up-market gym was busy with the usual fitness freaks, many of whom he knew. A couple of new ladies, in figure-hugging Lycra, had made the 45 minute workout pass faster than usual. The occasional smile from the brunette gave promise of a possible encounter in the future, but today he didn't have time to fraternise. After a twenty-minute swim he showered and got dressed. The trainers, jogging pants and T-shirt he'd arrived in, were stuffed in his locker. Now, dressed in a three piece tailored suit; blue shirt and silk tie, he looked more like a banker than one of the London heavy-mob.

He took the tube to Westminster and, after fighting his way through the crowds of tourists, came out across the road from the Houses of Parliament. He deftly negotiated the busy traffic and arrived at the Public Entrance to the seat of government a little before 2pm.

He gave his name and driving licence to the police officer in the gate-house. 'I have a meeting with Sir Anthony Fairfax.'

The officer checked his computer, then handed Black a VISITOR badge. 'Just follow the signs, sir. The Terrace Restaurant is clearly marked.'

Donny hung the badge around his neck. 'Cheers.' He quickly made his way inside and arrived at the Maître d's lectern just as Big Ben chimed two o'clock.

'Good afternoon, sir.'

'Afternoon. I'm meeting Sir Anthony Fairfax.'

'Of course, sir. This way please.'

Fairfax was seated at a table overlooking the river. 'Your lunch guest, Sir Anthony.'

'Thank you, Fletcher. Give us a few minutes would you?'

Black sat down. He didn't like Fairfax and thought him an arrogant freeloading snob. He frequented several of the clubs and casino's Donny operated and never ever paid for drinks, meals, or any other services, he regularly requested.

Purposefully not using the man's title, he said, 'Thanks for meeting me.'

'I wasn't keen on meeting you at all, Mr Black. But you insisted it was extremely serious and urgent. I only hope your definition of urgent is the same as mine.'

Donny looked around the restaurant, then leaned a little closer over the table. 'I've been approached by someone and offered a deal.'

Fairfax took a sip of water. 'A deal . . . I do wish you people would talk in plain English.'

Black frowned. *And I wish I could punch you in the fucking face you arsehole,* he thought. 'Maybe I should just go straight to The Red Queen. Cut you lot out altogether?'

Sir Anthony removed his spectacles and placed them on the table. 'Very well. I'm listening.'

Following his brief lunch with Donny Black, Sir Anthony immediately called Lord Valentine. 'We need to talk, Edward. Something serious has come up. Are you free to meet?'

'I do have a meeting in twenty minutes but, if it's urgent, come up now.'

The oak-panelled office had the faint smell of rich leather and furniture polish. The view from the windows looked down into Parliament Square, where Winston Churchill's formidable statue stood watch.

Valentine was at the window when his gofer entered. 'You said it was urgent, Anthony?'

'Yes, Your Lordship. I've just had a meeting with our friend, Mr Black.'

'Ah, yes, that rough chappie from the security company.'

'Yes. And it's not good.'

Fifteen minutes later Donny Black's and Deputy Commander Thomas Morrison's phones simultaneously pinged incoming messages.

Black swiped his screen. As he read the text he grinned and said quietly. 'Right.'

A few minutes later Morrison read the same text. A deep frown across his forehead.

Midnight tonight. Kensington Casino.

Chapter Thirty Eight
'Where The Hell Is Whitby'

The *Kensington Casino* was one of several operated by Lena Stavos's organisation. The ones in London however were decidedly more upmarket than those in Birmingham, Manchester and Glasgow. That said, the provincial operations still delivered a high turnover and more importantly as far as The Red Queen was concerned, provided diverse outlets for the laundering of vast amounts of illegal money.

Midweek was never as busy as the weekend, but the *Kensington* still managed to entice a regular clientele of Chinese and East European punters. Many of whom came, not only for the gambling but, for other 'services' available to those with the ability to pay.

The casino had several VIP rooms and it was in one of these the meeting was held. An elegant second floor room with Roulette; Blackjack tables; a small but well-stocked bar and a comfortable seating area. On the wall was a large screen TV.

Donny Black and the Turzo twins were already there, enjoying the courtesy bar, when Commander Thomas Morrison arrived. It was a few minutes after midnight when Lord Edward Valentine and Sir Anthony Fairfax showed up.

'What the hell's going on?' asked a worried looking Morrison.

'All in good time, Tom,' said Sir Anthony.

Lord Valentine's phone rang. 'Hello, my dear . . . Yes, all here.' He hung up.

'Well?' said Morrison.

As he took his seat on the big chesterfield, Valentine said, 'Could someone turn on the TV, please.'

The big screen came to life and Lena Stavos appeared. 'Good evening, gentlemen.'

Morrison and Fairfax sat down. Black and the Turzos stood behind the big leather couch, facing the screen.

'Hello, Lena,' said Valentine.

'I hope you don't mind if I conduct this meeting in-absentia, but I think it's prudent, in light of what is to be discussed.'

'And that is?' said Morrison.

'I think we should let Mr Black tell us,' said The Red Queen.

Morrison stood up and pointed to the Turzos and Black. 'Before we go any further, and no offence intended, but why are the hired help here? This is supposed to be a board-level meeting, is it not?'

'Sit down please, Commander. We'll decide who is present, not you,' said Lord Valentine.

'Yes, Tom,' added a smarmy Fairfax, 'you are not much more than hired help, as you so crudely put it, yourself. You've been with us a little over eighteen months. And although you have been exceedingly useful, you should know your place. Now sit down, please.'

Morrison's scowl was not lost on the group. As he resumed his seat he mumbled something.

'You had a comment, Tom?' said Fairfax.

The commander shook his head.

'Now. Can we please proceed?' said Stavos. 'Mr Black, if you would.'

Donny moved his position to the side, so all could see. He took a swig from the bottle of beer, then placed it on the table. 'Err, yeah. Right. So, a few days ago I was called to quote on a security job at a new office complex. That was just to get me there. The meeting I found, was with Bobby Stone. Shackleton Blister, Shack, as he now calls himself.'

The Turzos looked at each other and grinned, obviously amused at the name.

'To cut a long story short, he said they have crucial evidence on our operations. Evidence that can hit all of us.' He made a sweeping gesture with his hand.

'They? said Morrison.

Black frowned. 'What?'

'You said, they. Who are, they?'

'Okay, right. There were two women with him. One called Caroline. He was in *Idols* with her last week. And another, mixed race chic, Caribbean type. Never seen her before. She was the one that got me to the office complex. Said her name was Karen, but that's probably bullshit.'

Lord Valentine cleared his throat, clearly not enamoured by the vulgarity.

'Sorry, Yeah. Probably fake names.'

'Go on, please,' said Fairfax.

'They said if I were to flip, then I could get a deal.'

Lord Valentine frowned. 'Excuse me. Flip?'

'Flip, yeah. If I were to turn Queen's evidence.'

'Ah, yes. Please, continue.'

'They went on about having all the low-down on the operations; the car-wash money- laundering; the clubs;

who was involved. The full Monty. So, I said I would go along with it. Said I'd cooperate.'

'And what did they want you to do next?' said Morrison.

'Wait to be contacted.'

'Okay, thank you, Mr Black. That was all very interesting.' said Stavos.

The group's attention turned back to the big screen.

Lena continued. 'We must now decide our next move, gentlemen.'

'That's easy, boss. We just take 'em all out,' said a grinning Leon Turzo.

The Red Queen frowned. 'Whereas I do usually appreciate your ability to resolve a problem, Leon. I think this one needs a little more finesse. Especially if they have evidence that could materialise if anything were to happen to them.'

Morrison stood up. 'I agree. We need to be smart here. But there are a couple of things that concern me.'

Sir Anthony, a smarmy grin on his face, said, 'Oh, and what might concern you, Tom?'

The commander pointed to Donny Black. 'How do we know this guy is on the level? Why's it taken so long for him to bring this to us? How do we know he's not playing us?'

Black was about to speak, when Stavos said, 'I think we know he's being straight with us, Commander.'

Morrison turned back to the screen. 'We do? Really?'

Lena nodded slowly, the slightest of smiles on her face. 'This is not America. Anyone in witness protection over there might end up running a very nice hotel on the beach in Florida. This is Britain. If anyone is foolish enough to turn Queen's evidence, and enter witness protection, the best they could hope for would be a small bed and breakfast in Whitby. That is assuming they were still alive of course.'

Leon turned to his brother. 'Where the hell is Whitby?' he whispered.

The Red Queen continued. 'And I don't see our good friend and colleague, Mr Black here, wanting to throw away his very pleasant and extremely lucrative life here in London to live, if he actually did live, in the wilds of North East England.'

Lord Valentine stood up. 'So, what's our next move, Lena?'

For several second she said nothing . . . then, 'This, gentlemen is what we're going to do.'

Chapter Thirty Nine
'You Called Me Amanda'

The minimum of pleasantries were exchanged, and the *Kensington* meeting broke up a little after 1am. Lord Valentine and Sir Anthony left in the peer's Bentley, leaving Commander Morrison to find his own transport home. The Turzo brothers elected to stay and play roulette in the main casino. Not that they were avid gamblers, more because of their fondness for the very attractive, and extremely accommodating, hostesses.

Donny Black considered staying on as well, but the relationship between himself and the Turzos was not that cordial, so he bid them goodnight and left. It took a little while to find a cab at that hour of the morning, but he still managed to get back to his flat well before 2am.

Once home he poured himself a large vodka, then sat down to consider the evening's events. After a second shot of vodka, he picked up his phone and scrolled the contacts. He took a deep breath and swiped the screen.

The call was answered immediately. 'Okay, they've gone for it.'

Shack nodded at the ladies as he listened to Black. 'So, what's their plan, Donny?'

'They'll be coming for you. That arsehole, Tom Morrison, will show up with a warrant. They plan to take you to Lena Stavos's place in Buckinghamshire. They want the evidence.'

'Warrant for who?'

'Not sure.'

'Okay. Will you be out there?'

'Yeah.'

'Who else?'

'The whole mob. Stavos, Lord bloody Valentine and that faggot Fairfax.'

'What about muscle?'

'Those two psychos, the Turzo brothers, for sure. Morrison will probably have at least one of his bent guys as well, I suppose. Don't know what other heat Stavos has out there.'

'Okay, good. You're being smart, Donny. Don't mess it up now. Stick to the plan and you can walk away in good shape.'

'Yeah, but I lose the business.'

'You'll still have the money you've got stashed, and you'll be alive. You can go abroad. Go live the high-life in Thailand or somewhere.'

'Thailand! Jesus, with all those slanty-eyed fuckers. No thanks.'

'And you'll be long gone before they know what happened.'

'Yeah, right. Let's bleedin' hope so.'

'Okay, see you in the morning. Night, Donny.'

'Yeah, right.'

The line went dead.

'So?' said Amanda.

'In the morning. They're coming in the morning.'

'How was the sleaze?'

Shack grinned. 'He sounded scared.'

'Good. It should focus him.'

'You sure you want to do this, Amanda?'

She frowned. 'Amanda?' You called me Amanda? You never call me Amanda.'

He went over and hugged her. 'I don't want anything to happen to you, Y'Ladyship.'

She looked into his eye. 'Yes.'

'Yes, what?'

'Yes, I want to do this. I have to do it for Samantha.'

Shack nodded and turned to Ruby. 'How about you, gorgeous? You sure?'

She winked. 'I'm sure. You don't think we're going to let you have all the fun, do you?' She opened her arms and continued. 'Don't I get a hug?'

'Anytime.'

It was almost 3am when Shack and Ruby arrived at Chalky White's apartment. As they entered, he said, 'Thought there'd been a problem. Everything okay?'

'Yeah, all okay for now. Chalky, this is, Ruby. Ruby, this is our new friend, Chalky White.'

Chapter Forty
'Very James Bond'

Wednesday morning saw the return of clear blue skies and, unlike the previous day, no threat of thunder. Not at least as regards the weather. Thunder was coming though, but not from the sky.

At 7:15, Amanda's doorbell rang. She looked through the spyhole and saw two men. She took a deep breath and opened the door. 'Hello?'

'Good morning. Miss Amanda Lang?'

'Good morning. Yes.'

The men flashed ID's. The older of the two said, 'Deputy Commander Morrison, this is, Detective Inspector Cole. Could we come in please, miss?'

'Err, what's this about?'

'Could we talk inside please, Miss Lang?'

She stood to one side and the men entered. 'A Deputy Commander and a Detective Inspector? They are rather high ranks for a house-call aren't they?'

'Normally yes, miss. But in times such as these we must use our resources as efficiently as possible.'

'Times like these?'

'Yes, miss. We're following up on certain lines of enquiry, and we've been advised you may be in possession of an illegal firearm.'

Amanda frowned, then shook her head slightly. 'I do not have an illegal firearm. And I'd like to know who would advise you otherwise?'

Inspector Cole stepped forward, clearly agitated. 'Have you got a shooter or not, love?'

'Love? I'm not your love, and I do not take kindly to your tone, Detective.'

Morrison took a piece of paper from his jacket and gave it to her. 'Search warrant.'

She looked at the document, then handed it back.

'If you are in possession of a gun, just tell us. You really don't want Inspector Cole here wrecking this lovely apartment. Do you?'

Amanda looked at the young detective, then sighed. 'First bedroom on the left. Bottom draw, in the chest.'

Cole grinned and headed to the bedroom. He returned a few moments later with an even bigger grin, and the gun in his hand. 'A nice little Walther automatic. Very James Bond.'

Morrison took the weapon, flicked out the magazine, checked the ammunition, then pushed the clip back in. 'You said you didn't have a gun. A fully loaded one at that.'

She went to her desk, opened the draw and removed an envelope. 'I said, I didn't have an illegal firearm.'

Morrison opened the envelope, then frowned as he read the document. 'Why would you, a journalist, have a special licence from the Home Secretary, Miss Lang?'

'That's my business, Commander. Now if there is nothing else, I'd like you to leave.'

'Shackleton Blister.'

'Sorry, what?'

'Is Shackleton Blister staying here?'

Amanda shook her head. 'No. Well he was, but he left yesterday. What do you want with him?'

'Do you know where he's gone?'

'He said he was going to see a couple of old friends. That's all I know.'

'Will he be coming back?'

'In a few days, yes.'

'Okay. Thank you, you've been very cooperative.'

'Good. Now, as I've already said, I'd like you to leave.'

'I'm sorry, miss, but we're going to have to ask you to come with us. There are several more questions we still need answering.'

'I've answered all your questions here. Why do I need to go anywhere?'

Morrison waved the Home Secretary's envelope. 'We need some time to corroborate this. So, please. Let's go.'

'Very well, but I think this is a great deal of time-wasting on all our parts.'

Cole took her arm and snapped. 'We'll be the judge of that, love. Let's go.'

Amanda looked the detective in the eyes. 'Please take your hand off me.'

'Let her go, Inspector.' Morrison turned and opened the door. 'Please.'

'Let me get my bag.'

Morrison nodded, then slipped the Walther and the envelope into his pocket. 'Ready?'

'Yes.'

'After you, Miss Lang.'

They left the apartment and headed east, out of Hammersmith, along the M4.

157

Amanda saw the signs for Brentford and said, 'Where are we going, Commander? We seem to be heading away from the city.'

Morrison turned and smiled. 'Not far, Miss Lang.'

Once past Hayes, they turned north onto the M25. 'Which station are we going to?'

Again the commander turned. 'As I said, not far now, miss,'

At the Kings Langley junction they turned off the Orbital and headed north west.

'We're going out of the city. What's going on?' Through the rear-view mirror, she caught sight of the detective's eyes. A stupid grin on his face. 'I said, where are we going?'

'Just relax, love. We'll be there soon,' said Cole.

'No. I don't think so. Just stop the car. Now!'

Morrison turned and snapped. 'Sit back and shut up.'

'I beg your pardon!'

He slipped a hand inside his jacket and drew out a 9mm automatic. He rested the weapon on the back of the seat, the black muzzle pointing directly at her.

Amanda recoiled at the sight of the gun. 'What the hell?'

'I said, sit back, Miss Lang.'

Chapter Forty One
'Invisible'

Ruby and Shack had spent what was left of Tuesday night at Chalky White's flat. Ruby had managed a few hours' sleep on the couch. Shack had spent a wakeful night in the big armchair. At 7am, he slipped quietly into the kitchen and put the kettle on. A few minutes later Ruby came in, followed soon after by Chalky.

'Oh, sorry, did I wake you two?'

Chalky shook his head. 'Not me. I've been lying awake for a while now.'

Ruby smiled. 'I heard you leave the lounge.'

'Right then, who wants tea?'

At seven-thirty, Shack's phone pinged an incoming message. He quickly swiped the screen, a serious look on his face. 'Okay, they've taken Amanda.'

'Does she say how many?' said Chalky.

'Two.'

Ruby saw how worried he looked and touched his arm. 'We'll get through this, baby. She'll be okay.'

'That's good trade-craft preparing draft messages,' said Chalky, 'Just one touch on the screen and we get some info.'

'Amanda's idea. They'll probably take her phone at some point. But now we know she's with two people. We've arranged a couple of code words as well. If she has the opportunity, she'll give us more intel.'

Chalky nodded. 'Not bad for a journalist.'

'She's a smart lady,' said Ruby.

The doorbell rang. Shack frowned. 'Expecting more guests, Chalky?'

As he left the kitchen, he winked. 'I am. Hang on a sec.'

Ruby and Shack heard voices, then some laughter. Chalky held open the kitchen door. 'Come in. Some friends of mine you should meet.'

The surprise on Shack's and Ruby's faces was evident. 'Shack, Ruby. This is Ron and Gary.'

For several seconds Shack stared at the two homeless-looking men in front of him. Then he smiled. 'Right. These guys are with you.' He offered his hand. 'Good to meet you, both.'

Ruby frowned. 'What? Who?'

'Let them get cleaned up first. Then we'll talk,' said Chalky. He turned back to the men. 'You know where the bathroom is.'

Gary nodded. 'Cheers, boss.'

Fifteen minutes, later Ron and Gary returned. But instead of the two down and out homeless creatures that came in earlier, there now stood a couple of very fit looking men in clean jeans and T-shirts.

Chalky smiled. 'You two smell better. You want anything?'

'No, we're okay. We had a couple of bacon rolls earlier.'

Ruby raised her hands. 'Stop! Just stop, please. Would somebody please tell me what is going on?'

160

Chalky stood in front of the fireplace, as if to give a lecture. The others took seats. 'It's a bit of a long story actually, Ruby. And I can't really give you too much.'

She frowned. 'Boss? The guys called you, boss.'

'Okay, I know you're aware of Operation Overwatch, the Home Secretary's initiative against high level corruption. Right?'

She nodded.

Chalky took a deep breath. 'Well there's another operation. Operation Hobo. It started with a meeting, almost a year ago now, in a village hall north of Hereford. The Home Secretary met secretly with twenty four men. Her protection detail was asked to wait outside during the briefing. Her plan was simple. She intended to fight the war on the streets, from the streets.'

Ruby shook her head. 'War? I don't understand.'

'There's a war raging in the UK. Right now. In all major cities and towns. Shootings, stabbings. All kinds of criminal activity. Drugs. Trafficking. You know this. You see it on the news every day.'

Again, she nodded.

'The Home Secretary put an initial team together of twenty four men. Men with experience of the streets. The most dangerous streets in the world. Kabul; Baghdad; Mogadishu. She needed guys that could survive in an urban war. And she found such men in Hereford.'

Ruby stood up. 'The Special Air Service is based at Hereford. So you guys are SAS?'

Chalky and his two friends smiled. 'Technically we're no longer SAS,' said Ron.

'We've all resigned from the regiment,' said Gary. 'Temporarily, of course.'

'And the plan, the operation, whatever you call it. Was to do what?'

'Become invisible. Then take the fight to the drug dealers, rapists, criminals, where they operate and thrive. On the streets.'

'Invisible? What does that mean?'

Gary stood up. 'When we came in, what did you think?'

'How do you mean?' said Ruby.

'What did you think we looked like?

'Err, yes, okay . . . homeless I guess.'

Gary nodded. 'People see a homeless person on the street, but they don't really see them. They're pretty much invisible, yeah? How many passers-by give a second look to a poor sod huddled in a doorway? Hardly any,' he waved his hands, as if performing a magic trick. 'Invisible.'

'So, you guys do what exactly?'

'Whatever we need to. We live out there three or four nights a week. We watch and engage where needed. Take out the drug dealers. Criminals. Whoever. The police can't cope, and they can't do what we do. We have a bit more leeway, shall we say. It's working, we make a difference. But only because we fight violence with violence. Our team was the first to be brought in.'

'The first?'

Chalky nodded. 'There are now over a hundred and twenty like us in London; Birmingham; Manchester and Leeds.'

'All from the SAS?'

'It's not strictly kosher to put the army on the streets of the UK. But as we're technically retired, we're no longer

British Army. We serve at the pleasure of the Home Secretary.'

Ruby shook her head. 'This is unbelievable.'

'Why?' said Shack.

'I mean in a good way. For us, I mean. We start off with a vagrant and a one-eyed drunk, no offence, Shack.'

He grinned. 'None taken, love.'

'And now, we have three SAS tough guys . . . and a one-eyed drunk.'

They all laughed. Then Shack's phone beeped, and the laughter stopped.

Chapter Forty Two
'What Do You Want?'

It was almost nine o'clock, when Detective Inspector Cole stopped at the gates of the Red Queen's estate. A sign at the side of the entrance read *STAVOS STUD*. He grinned at the sexual connotation. A young guy came out of the small gatehouse. 'Good morning,' his thick Polish accent was evident.

Morrison leaned across. 'Thomas Morrison. We're expected,' he said.

The man nodded and went back into the gatehouse. A second or two later, the big gates swung open. They drove onto the estate, then carried on along the tree-lined driveway. A hundred yards in, the road forked. To the left was the Stavos mansion, to the right the stables, exercise areas and outbuildings.

Morrison pointed to the right. 'That way.'

'This is some place,' said Cole, clearly impressed with the Red Queen's domain.

They drove a little way past the stables and came to a stop outside what appeared to be a warehouse facility. Several other vehicles were parked close by.

Cole jumped out and quickly opened the back door. 'Okay, love, let's go.'

Amanda stepped out and looked at Morrison, the gun still in his hand. He waved the big automatic towards the entrance. 'That way please, Miss Lang.'

She took a deep breath and followed Cole inside, Morrison behind her. They passed through a small entrance hall with a couple of doors on each side. A larger, sturdier portal gave entrance to the main warehouse. 'In there,' said Morrison.

Cole opened the big door and the three entered. The interior was about the size of a tennis court and clearly used for storage. Banks of shelving along the side walls were stacked with boxes of various sizes. Several large packing cases on pallets filled the central area. At the far end of the facility were two large double doors. Daylight came in via the dozen or so skylights in the roof. A small desk, with a couple of chairs, was situated to the right of the door they'd just come through. On the desk were a computer and a phone.

The Turzo brothers, along with Donny Black, stood by the desk. Amanda's eyes met Black's. She caught the faintest of smiles from the big man. The twins looked at each other, then leered at Amanda.

Sir Anthony Fairfax was seated behind the desk. 'Ah, good morning, Miss Lang. Kind of you to join us.'

Morrison pulled out a chair. 'Have a seat.'

She sat down, then looked him in the eyes. 'Okay. This is obviously nothing to do with the police. So, what is it? Kidnapping?'

Cole flashed his stupid grin. 'Kidnapping? No, but not a bad idea, love.'

Morrison glared at the detective. 'Shut the fuck up.' He turned to Amanda. 'All we need from you is the evidence.'

She shook her head slightly. 'Evidence? I have no idea what you're talking about.'

Morrison stepped closer and slapped her hard across the face, the sound resonated around the warehouse. Her head was thrown back with the impact. She sucked in a deep breath; fought the urge to cry. She put a hand to her cheek. 'What the hell do you want?'

Morrison raised his hand again.

'That's enough, Commander!' snapped Fairfax. He came around the desk and stood in front of her. 'This can be very easy or extremely difficult for you, Amanda,' he smiled, the shark-like eyes, soulless. 'May I call you, Amanda?'

She continued to hold her cheek. 'I said, what do you want?'

'We're aware you are in possession of certain evidence. Evidence gathered by your late departed partner, Samantha.'

At the mention of Sam's name, the urge to cry was too much and a tear rolled down her cheek. Fairfax took out a crisp white handkerchief and offered it to her. She ignored the gesture and wiped away the teardrop with her fingers. 'Yes. There is some information.'

'Good. You are being very sensible, my dear. Now if you could provide us with that information, all this unpleasantness will be over.'

She sniffed and wiped her nose with the back of her fingers. 'It's in a safe-deposit. I'll have to go to the bank.'

Donny Black stepped forward. 'You can get your friend Shack to go for it, can't you?'

Fairfax looked at the big man, then back to Amanda. 'Is that possible, my dear?'

She looked at the men. All eyes were on her. 'I'll need to make a call.'

'Amanda. Morning, love. How're you doing?'

Ruby and the three SAS guys, their faces stern, listened to the speaker-call.

'Shack, I need you to go to the bank.'

'The bank? Why, what's up?'

'I'm with some people and they want Sam's information.'

'People? What people? What's going on? Are you okay?'

Ruby smiled slightly at Shack's feigned concern.

'Yes, I'm fine. But I need you to bring the contents of box 2-0-7 here.'

'2-0-7 . . . I . . .'

'I said . . . two, zero, seven, Shack. Just do as I ask, please. You know the access code.'

The frown on Shack's face was not lost on the others in the apartment. 'Okay, love. Where do I bring the stuff?'

'They'll send you instructions. Just make sure you leave in the next five or six minutes.'

The line went dead.

Shack looked at the others, the frown still present.

'What's wrong?' said Chalky, 'that's what we wanted, wasn't it?'

Shack didn't answer.

'What is it?' said Ruby.

'Yeah, sorry. Err, yeah, it's what we wanted.'

She put a hand on his arm. 'So, what's the problem?'

'The deposit box. 2-0-7. That's not the box with the evidence.'

'But you said you went with her to the bank and . . .'

'Yeah, I went with her, but we opened box one zero seven. Not 2-0-7.'

Chalky grinned. 'Trade-craft, mate. She's got two boxes. And I'll bet you a pound to a pinch of shit, the stuff in the second box is of no use. Smart woman.'

Shack nodded. 'Yeah. But why didn't she tell me before?'

Chalky shrugged. 'Who knows? So, what's the deal?'

'They're sending instructions. Oh, and there are six people with her.'

Again, Chalky grinned. '*Leave in five or six minutes*, the code to say how many are with her.'

Shack nodded. Yeah. Okay, I'll get to the bank. I'll be in touch as soon as they send me the location.'

'Hang on,' said Chalky, 'before you split we've got something for you.'

Shack turned back. 'Oh yeah?'

Chalky nodded to Ron and Gary. The two men stood up from the small couch, moved it away from the window, then rolled up the rug. Ron knelt down and took a flick-knife from his pocket. The blade clicked as it sprung out. The others watched as he deftly removed several floorboards. He leaned down and reached into the cavity. Chalky winked at Shack, as the first gun was produced. Two Uzi sub-machine guns followed. Then a Glock automatic; a sawn-off shotgun and two silenced Berettas. Finally, a dozen boxes of ammunition were all neatly placed on the floor.

Ron stood up and brushed a little dust from his jeans. 'That's the lot, boss.'

Shack, his mouth open, looked at the weapons. 'Jesus Christ!'

Chapter Forty Three
'Roger That'

The text, with instructions and location, arrived a few minutes after Amanda's call. Shack forwarded the same message to Chalky's phone, then hugged Ruby. 'See y'later, doll.'

She held onto him for a while, then touched his cheek. 'Be careful, baby.'

Chalky held out his hand. 'Good luck.'

Shack nodded. 'Cheers, mate.' He turned to Ron and Gary. 'See you guys later . . . I hope.'

Ron slapped him on the back. 'We'll be there. Don't worry.'

Gary gave a thumbs up. 'Rock-n-roll.'

The drive to the bank was tedious, due to the busy morning traffic, but by a quarter to eleven Shack was at last on his way to Buckinghamshire. Box two-zero-seven had been accessed using the same code as 107. The contents now resided in a small backpack on the seat next to him. *Why didn't she say there were two boxes?* he thought to himself.

He'd been reluctant to take a weapon, as he knew they'd almost certainly search him. The SAS lads however had convinced him to take the sawn-off shotgun, which was now concealed under the driver's seat. Shack remembered Chalky's comment. 'If it's discovered, then fair enough. If not, it's another asset should we need it.'

The drive around the M25 was a lot better than he'd hoped and, once north of the orbital, he made good time. When the SATNAV declared '*your destination is five hundred yards ahead*' he pulled over to the side of the road. He took a small plastic box from the pocket of the backpack and opened it. After activating the tiny device, he fitted it into his ear. The microphone, no bigger than a shirt button, was concealed behind his eye-patch. He cleared his throat and said, 'Monday, Tuesday, Wednesday.'

Almost immediately, Chalky's voice came back. 'Thursday, Friday, Saturday.'

Shack smiled, then drove back onto the road. It was twelve-thirty when the Audi pulled up to the gates of *STAVOS STUD*. Two men were now stationed at the gatehouse. They both came out as he approached. He lowered the driver's window and smiled. 'Shackleton Blister.'

No smiles were returned.

The older of the two said, 'Out, please,' then proceeded to pat him down.

The younger went to the car and gave it nothing more than a cursory glance inside, not even bothering to check the backpack. Shack smiled slightly at the lack of professionalism. The vehicle's boot was opened, then some words in Polish were exchanged. Shack got back in and started the engine.

The older man picked up the backpack, then slipped into the passenger seat. He turned to Shack and grinned. Several gold teeth glinted in the afternoon sun. 'Okay, we go.'

As they approached the fork in the drive, Shack said, 'Which way?'

The man pointed to the right.

Shack nodded. 'We're going to the stables.'

The man looked at him and pointed again. 'This way, this way.'

As they arrived at the stables, Shack said, 'Here?'

The man frowned and waved his hand. 'You go more ahead.'

A few moments later they pulled up at the warehouse. 'Are we going into this warehouse?'

The man was clearly annoyed now and snapped. 'Too much talking. Inside, now.'

The sound of Chalky's voice, in Shack's ear, was comforting. 'Warehouse. Roger, that.'

The white van pulled up to the big gates. The sign on the side read *City Plumbing Services*.

The young Polish guard came out and glared at the driver. 'What you want?'

Ron leaned out of the window and smiled. 'Stavos Stud? We got an emergency call-out, mate.'

'You wait. I check.'

The guard turned, but never knew what hit him. He fell against the side of the van, then slithered to the ground. Gary stood over him and grinned. 'I remember the Poles being a lot tougher.'

Chalky rushed around the van and helped carry the unconscious guard back into the gatehouse. It took less than twenty seconds to secure his hands and feet with cable-ties. Gaffer tape was fixed firmly over his mouth.

They rolled him onto his stomach and pushed him under the small counter. 'He's going nowhere,' said Gary.

Chalky winked, then threw the switch to open the gates. As the van drove through, they both jumped into the back.

Chapter Forty Four
'Sussed It Yet?'

The heat in the warehouse had become rather oppressive and Sir Anthony had asked for the double doors, at the end of the building, to be opened. The slight breeze coming in did give some relief, but not much.

As Shack and the guard entered, Fairfax stood up. 'Ah. At last.'

Shack quickly looked around. Then said to Amanda. 'Are you okay?'

'She's fine,' said Morrison. He used his gun to point to the desk. 'Bag on the table.'

Fairfax turned to the guard. 'Thank you. You can go.'

The man stood his ground. 'Is okay. I stay.'

Leon Turzo stepped forward and snapped at the security man in Polish. Without a word the guard turned and left.

Detective Cole took out his automatic. 'You took your time getting here.'

Shack shrugged. 'I left in six minutes.'

The voice in his ear said, 'Six. Copy that.'

Cole came forward, grabbed hold of Shack's arm and pulled him away from the desk. 'Over here, one-eye.'

Shack yanked his arm away and glared at the detective. Cole stuck his gun into Shack's side. 'I said, over here, arsehole.'

Fairfax emptied the contents of the backpack onto the desk. 'Now what have we here?'

'So, just the hired help here today,' said Shack, to no one in particular.

Cole pressed the muzzle hard into Shack's ribs. 'Shut the fuck up.'

'The Red Queen not joining us? No Lord Valentine?'

Again. 'Copy that,' from the earpiece.

Cole rapped the back of Shack's head with the barrel of the gun. ' Keep talking. See what's next.'

Amanda jumped up. 'Leave him alone!'

Morrison grabbed her arm and twisted it behind her back. 'Shut up.'

Shack rubbed the back of his head, then looked at Donny Black. 'How're you doing, Donny?'

Cole raised his weapon again.

'Enough!' said Morrison.

Donny smiled. 'I'm fine me ol' mate. A lot better than you're going to be.'

Shack frowned. He looked into Black's eyes. The big man grinned, then he too produced a gun. 'You sussed it yet, Bobby? . . . Shack . . . whatever you call yourself now?'

Leon turned to Milosh and said quietly. 'What is susshed?'

Milosh shrugged.

Sir Anthony stood up from the desk. 'Well, well, well. Someone has been a busy little bee.' All eyes turned to him. 'Quite a cache of information here, Amanda. Your dear departed was very clever indeed.'

'So, what now?' said Morrison.

'I think it's time to say goodbye to our two friends here. Mr Black and the Turzo boys can take care of things from here.'

Donny stepped forward; his gun aimed at Shack. 'My pleasure,' he grinned, 'sorry, mate. Our deal is off. I don't fancy Whitby.'

Shack shook his head slightly, then looked at Amanda. Morrison stood close behind her, her arm still in his grasp at the back.

Fairfax returned the evidence to the rucksack. 'Wait until we go, then it's over to you, Mr Black.'

Morrison leaned close to Amanda's ear. 'Pandora,' he said softly.

She turned and looked at him. His nod was almost imperceptible. The armlock was released and she felt her Walther being placed in her hand, the steel cold in her sweaty palm.

'Safety is off,' he whispered. Then quickly he turned his weapon on Donny. 'Step back,' he ordered.

Sir Anthony frowned. 'Tom?'

Again, Morrison waved his gun. 'I said, step back! Nobody's getting rid of anybody.'

Donny lowered his gun and raised a hand. 'Okay, okay. Chill-out, mate.'

Detective Cole still had Shack covered, the surprise on his face evident. 'What the hell?'

'Shut up, Cole and drop your weapon. Both of you, guns on the floor. Now.'

Sir Anthony shook his head. 'Commander Morrison . . . Thomas. What do you think you are doing?'

'He's flipped!' shouted Black, 'they've got to him. He's fucking us.'

The crack of the gunshot echoed around the warehouse. Cole's bullet hit Morrison in the shoulder. He staggered backwards but returned fire, hitting the detective in the chest.

Donny Black raised his gun, but Amanda fired first. The three-round burst knocked him clear off his feet.

The Turzo brothers dived behind a large packing case and drew their weapons. Shack lunged at Amanda knocking her to the floor. Together they rolled behind the desk.

The Turzos opened fire.

Bullets smashed into the desk and stone floor. Dust and chunks of concrete filled the air. It was impossible to return fire from their position. All Shack and Amanda could do was keep their heads down.

The desk was splintering all around them as the withering fire from the Turzos chewed up their only protection.

Then more gunfire. This time from halfway down the warehouse. The distinctive high-pitched rattle of their Uzis, as Ron and Gary poured 600 rounds a minute into the brothers' position.

'Okay, okay. Enough!' The Turzos threw out their weapons and raised their hands.

The two SAS men ran forward, their smoking Uzis trained on the brothers. Donny Black and Detective Cole lay on the blood-splattered concrete. Commander Morrison was unconscious and looked to be losing a lot of blood.

Amanda and Shack knelt beside him. She checked the wound, then his pulse. 'We need to get him to a hospital.'

Gary felt for vital signs on Cole and Black. 'These guys are gone.' He took a field-dressing from his body armour and expertly dressed Morrison's wound. 'He'll be okay. The round's still in there, but he'll be okay.'

Shack stood up. 'Where the hell is Fairfax?'

The door swung open and Sir Anthony entered, followed by a smiling Chalky. 'He's here.'

Chapter Forty Five
'Ten Days Later'

Normally the drive, from Hammersmith to SW1 in a black cab, could take anything up to three quarters of an hour. But, with flashing blue lights and an extremely cavalier driver, the Special Branch Jaguar made the journey in less than 15 minutes.

Shack was seated between Amanda and Ruby in the back of the elegant motor. At eleven-fifteen the car stopped at the security barrier of *Number Two Markham Street*. The Special Branch officers flashed their ID's to the heavily-armed guard, who turned and nodded to his colleague in the security box. A moment or two later, the 3 big steel bollards sank into the ground. Shack smiled as the Jag was waved through to the underground parking of the Home Office.

Amanda, Ruby and Shack were cleared through security and given VISITOR badges. The Security Officer pointed behind them. 'Here's your escort now.'

A young woman approached. 'Ah, good you're all badged up,' she smiled. 'Good morning. I'm Elizabeth, the Home Secretary's Senior PA. So good to have you here today. We can go right up.'

The three followed the woman into the lift. 'Nice building,' said Shack.

'Yes, but it does lack some character.' The lift pinged. 'Here we are.'

As they stepped out several people looked at them, some clearly interested in the man with the eye-patch.

The PA smiled again. 'This way.'

They passed through a couple of outer offices, then stopped at a set of double doors.

Shack ran his fingers through his hair and winked at Ruby.

Elizabeth knocked. 'Come in,' came the reply.

'Miss Lang, Miss Brennan and Mister Blister, are here, Home Secretary.'

As they entered the smartly dressed woman stood up and came round the big desk. 'Thank you, Elizabeth,' she said.

'Ma'am.'

The Home Secretary smiled as she shook hands. 'So very nice to meet you. Please, let's have a seat. Now, how are you all? It's been ten days since your little escapade in Buckinghamshire, and very remiss of me to not have met with you before now.'

'I think we are all fine now, thank you, ma'am,' said Amanda.

Shack and Ruby smiled and nodded affirmation.

'Good, that's good. You certainly presented as a formidable team. I have of course read all the reports and your actions have contributed enormously to subsequent events in Operation Overwatch.'

Shack nodded. 'Yes, ma'am. The newspapers certainly had a feeding frenzy once the scale of the problem was known.'

The Home Secretary frowned. 'Yes, the media does tend to revel in such news. No offence Amanda, you being a journalist and all that.'

'None taken, ma'am.'

'The results of Overwatch certainly were rather shocking to be honest. Over one hundred and forty senior police officers in London; Birmingham; Manchester and Leeds, arrested and charged. Several senior people in the government arrested and charged. Not to mention various elements of the organised crime syndicate. Thanks to the sensible cooperation of Lord Valentine, we now have a full picture of who was responsible for what.'

Shack shook his head slightly. 'Yes, Valentine definitely managed to dodge a bullet by turning Queen's evidence.'

The Home Secretary stood up and went to her desk. 'Indeed, he has avoided prison, but he is certainly ruined. His peerage will be revoked, and his money and property confiscated as proceeds of crime.'

'Sorry, ma'am but I doubt you'll be able to access his overseas accounts,' said Amanda.

'That's true, but let's see.' She returned to the couch and handed Shack a large envelope.   'We owe you three a great deal. And you, Shack . . . well, this may not change the past and will do nothing to replace what you've lost. But it may help with your future.'

He took the envelope and carefully ran his finger along the flap. The others sat silently as he read the document. He looked up and said, 'Thank you, ma'am.'

'Well?' said Ruby, 'don't keep us in suspense.'

He handed the paper to her, Amanda moved closer and read out loud. 'Total exoneration for the death of Chrissy. Criminal record expunged. Apologies and thanks from a grateful government.'

The Home Secretary, turned to Amanda. 'Nothing we can do will bring Samantha back. But if you will allow me, I intend to recommend her for a posthumous award for gallantry?'

Amanda smiled and nodded.

'Good.' She looked at her watch. 'Now . . . I have a meeting with the American Ambassador at two. But that still leaves us plenty of time for our lunch.'

Shack grinned. 'As long as I can have a beer, ma'am?'

The Home Secretary laughed. 'I'm sure we can provide you with a suitable beverage.'

They all stood up.

There was a knock at the door. 'Come in.'

Elizabeth entered. 'Excuse me, ma'am. Deputy Commander Morrison is here.'

'Ah, excellent. Right on time.'

Elizabeth stepped aside as Morrison entered, his left arm in a sling.

'Good afternoon, Home Secretary.'

'Thomas. Good to see you again. You know everyone here?'

He nodded, then shook hands with Shack.

'How's the shoulder, Tom?' said Shack.

The commander frowned. 'Bloody sore.'

Ruby shook hands. 'Hello again.'

Amanda stepped forward and kissed his cheek. 'Hello, Tom.'

The Home Secretary cleared her throat. 'Right. Now we're all here, let's have some lunch.'

In the dining room, the Home Secretary took a seat at the head of the table. Her four guests sat down as the Head

Waiter handed out menus. 'Would you like the wine list ma'am?'

She smiled. Yes, please. Oh, and a beer.'

'Certainly ma'am.'

Amanda sat next to Morrison. 'Are you feeling better?' she said.

'Yes, I'm fine. Thank you. Going back to work next week.'

'That quick?'

'Afraid so. Much to do. A lot of things to sort out.'

'Yes. I suppose so.'

'How about you, Amanda? You're okay?'

'Yes, I think so. Now I know what happened to Samantha, and that those responsible will face justice.'

Morrison nodded. 'Yes . . . the Turzos brothers will be going away for rather a long time.'

'Good,' said Shack. 'And their stunt-driver friend?'

The commander nodded again. 'Her film career is over.'

'What about Sir Anthony Fairfax, Tom?' said Ruby.

The Commander smiled. 'I'll be especially pleased to see his smug face in the dock at the Old Bailey.'

The waiter returned. 'What can I get you, ladies and gentlemen? We have some beautiful turbot today.'

Lunch over, the Home Secretary got up. 'I'm sorry everyone, but duty calls and I really have to leave. You must stay for dessert though. The pastry chef here is quite a magician. Let the Maître d' know when you're ready to go and he'll get Elizabeth over to escort you out.'

They all stood and shook hands with her.

'Thank you, ma'am,' said Shack.

'No, thank you. Thank you all, for everything you've done.'

As the Home Secretary departed the waiter arrived. 'Would anyone care for dessert?'

Everyone smiled.

The desserts were as delicious as the Home Secretary had promised and a couple of bottles of wine, and a few more beers, finished off what was a most relaxing lunch. It was a quarter to three when Shack asked the head waiter to call Elizabeth.

Morrison poured the last of the wine. 'Well, ladies and gentleman. I have to say you certainly are a very capable bunch. And if I were to stay undercover, I think I'd be asking you to join me.'

'You really want us to answer that, Tom?' said Ruby.

'Well, perhaps not.'

They all laughed.

Shack leaned forward. 'There is one thing. We know it was the Turzo's stunt-driving friend who caused my accident and also killed Detective Bowen. And we now know it was Detective Cole who set me up to fail the alcohol test.'

Morrison nodded. 'Correct.'

'But how did he manage to do that?'

'Right, yes. There was an analyst in the Testing Lab. Had a drug problem. Cole used that against him and had your blood sample doctored.'

Shack shook his head slightly. 'The web gets bigger the more you dig.'

Morrison, a serious look on his face, nodded again. 'Yes, it does.'

Shack swallowed a mouthfull of beer. 'And it was you who tipped me off about being followed from the Masonic Hall.'

Morrison smiled. 'Yes, I sent the message. I'd been watching you guys, since you showed up at *Idols* that first night. But it was Captain Charles Whitehead, who had your back most of the time.'

'Who?' said Ruby.

'Charles Whitehead. Captain, Special Air Service.'

Shack raised his glass and smiled. 'Chalky White! Yes, okay. Nice one, Chalky. Cheers.'

Elizabeth arrived. 'Everyone ready to go?'

As they walked from the restaurant, Amanda turned to Morrison. 'There's one thing I'd like to ask as well, Tom.'

'Oh, yes?'

'In the warehouse, when you slipped me the gun. You said *Pandora.* How did you know I would understand what that meant?'

He smiled. 'To be honest, I didn't. But I hoped Samantha had told you that *Pandora*, was the codeword to identify anyone involved with Operation Overwatch.'

Chapter Forty Six
'A Stone In My Jimmy Choo'

In a very elegant dacha, a few miles south east of Moscow, Lena Stavos was raging. Her host, Sergei Ivanovich Borodin, watched as she paced back and forth like an angry panther. Her curses and profanities, spat out in Polish, were lost on him. He spoke some of her language, but not enough to keep up with her tirade.

Their common tongue was English. Borodin stood and took hold of her shaking hands. 'Lena, be calm. Sit down. Take some vodka. Let's talk. Think.'

She looked at the Russian. In his late sixties, he was still handsome. But his warm smile and charming demeanour belayed his true character. He was intelligent, ruthless and unforgiving. And since the fall of the Soviet Union, his business had grown. He now ran a mafia family second only to the infamous Kuragin's. Lena had worked with Sergei for over ten years and their interests in the UK were mutually beneficial.

'Yes . . . yes. You're right, Sergei. But how can I stay calm, when I can't go back to England? And my contacts back home tell me the Polish authorities are waiting for me to show up there. Bastards! I can't even go home.'

'Well you're safe here in Russia and you're welcome to stay as you long as you wish, darling.'

She touch his cheek. 'Thank you, Sergei.'

He poured two shots of vodka, then handed her one. He raised his glass. 'Nostrovia!'

She took a deep breath as the chilled fiery liquid hit her stomach. 'Ah, real vodka. Almost as good as our Polish.'

He grinned and poured two more shots. 'Now. Let's talk about your problem, darling.'

It was almost an hour later when Lena Stavos finished outlining the full extent of her problems. The Home Secretary's undercover operation had infiltrated her organisation. The drug and money laundering, through her car-wash and casino businesses, had been exposed. The network of corrupt police officers, built up over many years, destroyed. And the exposure of several government figures she'd had on her payroll, was the final straw.

It became abundantly clear to Borodin she'd been extremely fortunate to have slipped out of the UK before being arrested herself. 'You were smart to leave when you did, Lena. But the question is, what do you intend to do next? And what do you want from me?'

They'd consumed the first bottle of vodka and a second had been opened. Although she felt a little lightheaded, The Red Queen was still in control of her faculties. 'Firstly, I'm not going to drink any more of this.' She pushed her glass away and stood up.

Sergei grinned and got up. 'Yes, of course. Why would you? It's not as good as Polish.'

She smiled at his little jibe. 'What I intend to do, my Russian friend, is remove a stone from my Jimmy Choo.'

'And who might this stone be?'

She frowned. Her eyes narrowed. 'Lord Edward Valentine has decided to save his own ass and turn state's evidence.'

'Queen's evidence.'

'What?'

'It is called Queen's evidence in the UK.'

She raised her hand in a throw away gesture. 'Whatever. But that bastard will not get away with betraying me.'

'And you need my help with this Valentine?'

'I do, my dear Sergei.'

He poured another vodka, swallowed it, then said, 'Hmm, I think I may have the solution.'

'Yes?'

He shouted, 'Sasha!'

A few seconds later a young man entered. 'Da, boss?'

'Sasha. Contact Draco.'

Chapter Forty Seven
'It's Been Fun'

Almost a month had passed since Shack and Amanda had travelled down to London. The last few days, after the Home Secretary's meeting, had been spent enjoying the city. The papers were still milking the stories of bent cops and corrupt government officials, all of which were far more entertaining than the Brexit debacle. Amanda had written several pieces for various tabloids. But now it was time for Shack and Ruby to get back to Manchester.

Amanda had insisted she drive them to Euston and pulled into the drop-off zone a little before 11am. After unloading the bags, she hugged Ruby. 'Stay in touch, darling. Come down anytime. You're always welcome.'

Cheeks were kissed. 'Same to you,' said Ruby, 'but Manchester might be a bit too quiet for you, after the last few weeks.'

They laughed.

Amanda turned to Shack and kissed his cheek. 'Have a good trip. Call me when you get back.'

He put his arms around her and held on for several seconds. 'Will do. Thanks for everything, Y'Ladyship. It's been fun.'

She watched until they disappeared into the station, then murmured quietly, 'Take care, partner.'

At twenty past eleven, the barrier at platform 13 opened. Ruby and Shack made their way along the crowded platform, to the front of the train, and climbed aboard the

First Class carriage. The coach was filling up, and the man with one eye attracted several glances as they found their seats.

Shack's carrier clunked, when he placed it on the table. He sat down and took out Ruby's magazine and newspaper. A bottle of water and four small cans of *Gordons Gin & Tonic*, came next, followed by a four-pack of Stella Artois.

She smiled and tapped the cans. 'It's only two hours to Manchester. Will you have enough?'

'Hmm, maybe not.' He grinned. 'But they have a buffet on here.'

As the train pulled out of the station, she picked up the magazine and shook her head. 'That's my boy.'

Chapter Forty Eight
'Katarina'

Edward Valentine was, to all intents and purposes, under house arrest. He'd been fitted with a tag and was subject to a strict curfew. He was allowed to walk his dogs, in the park across from his London pied-à-terre, but that was it.

His wife had left him the day after he lost the knighthood and moved in with their daughter in Hampshire. The money in his UK bank accounts had been confiscated, under the Proceeds of Crime Act. The big house in the country had already gone, along with his Bentley and classic Jaguar. The London house would soon be auctioned off.

All he had left were his two spaniels. Both of which his wife hated, otherwise they would now be in Hampshire as well. Everything had gone, in exchange for testifying against the bent cops and corrupt government officials involved with the Red Queen's organisation. They'd taken everything, or so they thought. But with over one and a half million in his Montenegro bank account, Valentine knew his future would not be too dismal.

There was a light drizzle this morning and the park was quieter than normal. The dogs though, seemed excitable for some reason and they pulled and tugged at their leads as they played with each other. 'Come on now, boys. Calm down.'

The woman jogging towards him was beautiful, in her late thirties, with a blonde pony-tail that swished back and forth as she ran. As she came closer he realised he was staring. The dogs were on the path, their leads all tangled. His eyes were fixed on the woman. Then she stumbled, caught up between the dogs.

'Oh, my goodness!' he blurted out, 'I'm so sorry.' He held onto her as the animals, the leads and her long legs, became more entangled.

She laughed and held onto him. 'It's okay, it's okay. No harm done.' Her long finger-nails caught the back of his hand, as he extricated her from the troublesome spaniels.

'Oh, my dear, I'm so sorry. These boys are out of control this morning.'

She smiled. 'No problem, I should have been more careful.'

He returned her smile. 'I haven't seen you here before. And your accent , Polish?'

She continued to smile, then bend down and stroked the playful dogs. 'No, I'm Russian, just visiting for a few days.'

She stood up and looked into his eyes. 'Okay . . . enjoy your walk.' She turned to the dogs. 'Bye, bye, boys.'

'Goodbye, my dear.' As she trotted off, his gaze was fixed on her buttocks. He took a deep breath. 'Hmm, that was very pleasant.' He rubbed the back of his hand, then licked the tiny scratch. 'Very pleasant indeed.'

* * *

The flight from London to Moscow was delayed by thirty minutes. Katarina Elena Draconova waited in the Business Class Lounge, a glass of champagne on the table

191

in front of her. The lounge was busy and almost all the passengers appeared to be Russian businessmen. A couple of whom had already made overtures, but her icy response had left them in no doubt she was not interested. Several television screens were positioned around the lounge and, although the sound was off, there was a written commentary at the bottom of the pictures.

The 6pm BBC News, filled the screen. After a short report on the latest Brexit issues, a story unfolded that made her smile. She read the transcript along the bottom of the screen, as the newsreader relayed the report. *The disgraced and former lord, Edward Valentine, was found dead this afternoon. Valentine had been under house arrest for some time, in relation to ongoing Home Office investigations into corruption. A neighbour was alerted by the continuous barking of Valentine's dogs. Police gained entry to the London home, just after 3pm. First reports indicate the cause of death was a heart attack.*

She picked up her phone and tapped out a message. In Moscow, Sergei Borodin's phone pinged an incoming. He swiped the screen and read the short message. *He is dead.*

Katerina dropped the phone into her bag, just as the loud-speaker announced. *Aeroflot 404 to Moscow Domodedovo, is now ready for boarding. Please proceed to gate seventeen.*

She picked up her glass and swallowed the last of the champagne. As she walked to the exit, she caught sight of herself in one of the long mirrors and smiled.

Chapter Forty Nine
'The Red Queen Strikes Back'

The Daily Mail's front page left nothing to the imagination. CORRUPT PEER FOUND DEAD.

Shack read the piece, then called Amanda. 'Morning, Y'Ladyship. How're you doing?'

'Good morning. I'm fine. Just off to the gym.'

'You seen the papers?'

'Not yet, but I saw the news. You mean Valentine?'

'Yeah . Heart attack, eh? And suddenly. Very strange.'

'Strange? Why? You think it was suicide?'

'No, not him. Why would he top himself? Okay he's finished here, but he's bound to have plenty stashed abroad.'

'Yes, I suppose.'

'And apparently he was fit as a butcher's dog.'

She smiled at his comment. 'So, you think it's retribution?

He grinned. 'The Red Queen strikes back. Sounds like a *Star Wars* episode.'

'Well, I'm sure we'll find out once the post-mortem is done.'

'Yeah, let's see. Okay, I'll let you get off to the gym. I'm going too.'

'Where? The gym?'

'Not likely, love. I'm off for a bacon sandwich.'

He heard her laugh. 'Bye, partner. Talk soon.'

'Bye, Y'Ladyship.'

Shack left his office and headed down to the café. The morning was overcast, but still warm, with a light breeze carving ripples across the waters of North Quay.

He saw Maria as he approached and gave a little wave. For a second or two she just stared, not returning the wave or even a smile, then went back inside. The café, as always at this time of the morning was busy. Shack went to a table at the edge of the walkway, next to the quayside. He was about to take his seat when Maria appeared, her arm outstretched. For a second Shack didn't realise what it was in her hand. Then the crack of the gunshot rang out.

The first bullet hit him high in the chest; shattered his clavicle and spun him around. The second round smashed into his back. The impact knocked him off the quayside and into the cold grey water.

Maria dropped the gun, the sound as it clattered to the floor was muted by the screams from the customers. Several instinctively fell to the ground, others knocked over tables and chairs as they ran from the café frontage. Maria slowly turned, as if in a trance, and began to walk away. Two men leapt at her; wrestled her to the ground. As the sound of sirens grew louder, she whimpered, 'I had to, I'm sorry, I had to . . .'

In the chilly waters of North Quay, Shack sank slowly into the darkness. Then Chrissy was there, her arms open wide, her smile as beautiful as ever. 'I'm waiting for you, Bobby . . . I'm here, my darling . . . I'm here.'

Chapter Fifty
'Lucky!'

The morning was warm, with a cloudless blue sky. The traffic slowed, then stopped, to allow the small convoy of cars to follow the hearse into the cemetery. At the entrance to the crematorium, a couple of dozen people waited for Shack to arrive. The group fell silent as the big black motor came to a stop. Funeral attendants helped lift his coffin onto the pall-bearer's shoulders. The music began, a soul tune from years ago, its melancholy notes filled the hall. A few mourners smiled in recognition. 'He loved this,' someone said.

The casket was gently placed on the dais; the bearers returned to their seats.

The minister cleared his throat. 'Good morning, everyone. We will begin with Shackleton's favourite hymn . . . Jerusalem.'

Chrissy and Shack stood, hand in hand, at the rear of the hall. He turned to her and smiled. 'I love you.'

She kissed him gently, then stepped back. He looked at her as she walked away. He shouted, 'Chrissy! . . . Chrissy! . . . Wait for me!'

Then she was gone. He shouted but his voice failed. The words wouldn't come out. He couldn't speak. Just a guttural sound from deep in his throat. 'Ahgggg!'

Amanda called out, 'Nurse! Nurse, he's waking up.'

Ruby stepped out of the way.

The nurse rushed in and touched Shack's hand. 'Stay calm. It's only the ventilator in your throat. Stay calm . . .we'll take it out now.'

Twenty minutes later, the extubating over, Amanda and Ruby came back in. The delight, at seeing him sitting up, evident on their smiling faces.

He sipped some water, then rubbed his good eye. 'What happened?'

Amanda took his hand. 'Do you remember anything?'

He frowned, took more water. 'Shot? Yeah, I was shot, right?'

Ruby kissed his cheek. 'Yes. At the café. The girl there.'

'Yeah, yeah, I remember . . . why?'

'Don't worry about that now,' said Amanda. 'The main thing is you're going to be fine.'

He touched the dressing on his shoulder. 'This?'

Ruby moved his hand away. 'Leave that. The bullet broke your collar bone. But they say it's healing nicely.'

He moved his shoulders. 'And my back?'

'Second one caught your shoulder blade. You were lucky,' said Amanda.

'Lucky?'

She smiled. 'Lucky to be alive, I mean. We've been worried for weeks.'

'Weeks?'

Ruby nodded and gently touched his cheek. 'You've been in a coma for over a month, baby.'

Chapter Fifty One
'Surprises'

Four days later, Shack was discharged. Ruby was insistent he stay with her for a few days and, despite his protestations, was adamant he was coming home with her. It'd been several years since a woman had looked after him; now he was set in his ways and used to doing his own thing. Nevertheless, the thought of Ruby's company was not unpleasant.

Amanda had returned to London but promised to come back up in a couple of weeks' time.

His wounds had healed nicely and once the current course of antibiotics was finished, he'd be off medication. A regime of gentle physiotherapy had been prescribed, to rebuild muscle tone in the damaged areas. Apart from that he fully intended to be back at work as soon as possible.

Shack had been at Ruby's for two days, when she announced, 'There's someone coming to see you this afternoon.'

'Here? Who?'

She kissed him. 'It's a surprise. In fact there could be a couple of surprises for you, baby.'

He grabbed her arm and pulled her to him, a big smile on his face. 'What're you up to, gorgeous?'

'Wait and see. They'll be here at three o'clock.'

'They?'

She wagged a finger. 'Oh, no. I said it's a surprise.'

At ten to three, the doorbell chimed. Ruby stood up. 'They're early.' She went to the door and returned a few moments later with two men. Shack's look of surprise brought a smile to her face.

'*Mister Brown*! What're you doing here?'

'Hello again, Shack. Good to see you looking so healthy. All things considered.'

'Have a seat gentlemen,' said Ruby, I'll bring some tea.'

'Anything stronger?' said Shack.

She headed to the kitchen. 'Maybe later.'

'Shack, this is my lawyer, Solomon Goldstein . . . Sol, this is Shackleton Blister.'

They shook hands. 'Very good to meet you, Shack.'

'Err, yeah . . . I guess so. What's going on?'

'May we sit?' said Goldstein.

'Yeah sure.'

The lawyer put his briefcase on the couch next to him, then flipped open the lid.

Ruby returned with the tea. 'Here we are.' Then she sat down next to Shack.

Goldstein took a drink, then smiled. 'Now, Shack, our mutual client, and friend here,' he gestured to *Mister Brown*, 'contacted me a few weeks ago. The Home Office's operation, and the shocking incident in Buckinghamshire of course, was all over the media. Your part along with that of Miss Brennan and Miss Lang, were significant in the exposure and apprehension of those involved,' he took another sip of tea. 'An enterprise, I must say, which was extremely daring on your parts.'

Shack frowned. 'Maybe too daring!'

Goldstein made a gesture with his hand. 'Perhaps . . . But to continue,' he removed some documents from his briefcase and put on his spectacles. 'The subsequent good news, for you, was the clearing of your name and total exoneration. That of course did nothing to assuage the loss of your family and the two very difficult years in prison.' The lawyer watched as Shack adjusted the eye-patch. 'Yes . . . another unfortunate legacy of that confinement. Then the terrible shooting in Salford Quays. From which I hope you are fully recovered?'

Shack nodded. 'I'll be fine.'

Ruby touched his knee and smiled.

'Get on with it, Sol,' said *Brown*. 'The poor guy's been through enough without having to listen to you rabbiting on!'

They all laughed.

'Yes . . . yes. I'm sorry. So, to get to the point. I was instructed, by our friend here, to act on your behalf. And to that end, put a very strong case to the Crown Prosecution Service and Home Office, for compensatory restitution.' He handed a document to Shack. 'With the resulting conclusion.'

Shack rubbed his good eye, then read the paper. He looked up at Ruby, then *Brown*. He turned to Goldstein. 'One million, two-hundred and fifty thousand pounds!'

The lawyer nodded. 'There is also the insurance.'

'Insurance?'

'Yes. As we now know, you were not responsible for the death of your wife. So I took the issue up with your insurance company.' Solomon handed him another document. 'This confirms the company's intention to honour the life-cover on Christine and a payment of three-hundred thousand pounds will be forthcoming.'

Shack, clearly stunned, said nothing. Ruby raised her hand and gently pushed his chin up. 'Your mouth's open, hon.

Several moments passed in silence. Then Shack turned to *Brown.* 'You arranged all this?'

Brown smiled, then nodded. 'I had help from Ruby and Amanda. But all the real work was done by Solomon, here.'

'But why would you do that for me? We don't really know each other.'

'Because you helped me. You were honest and discreet. And because you're a good man, Shack.'

Ruby stood up. 'Now we can have something stronger.'

After the footballer and the lawyer had gone, Ruby cleared away the tea tray. She topped up their glasses with the last of the champagne. She raised hers. 'Nothing's going to change the past, baby. But I think the future is going to be a little bit easier for you.'

They chinked glasses and swallowed down the sparkling liquid. He took her in his arms and kissed her. He was about to speak, when she put her finger to his lips. 'There's one more surprise.'

'What the . . .?'

She touched his lips again. 'You'll see,' she picked up her handbag and car keys, 'Let's go.'

Twenty minutes later, Ruby pulled into the underground parking of *The Cheshire,* one of the swish tower blocks at the north end of Salford Quays. They took the lift to the 8th floor and came out into a very stylish corridor.

She pointed to each door as they passed. 'There are only four apartments on each floor.'

At number 4 she tapped in the access code. Shack followed her in. 'How do you like it?' she said. 'Two bedrooms, both en-suite. Nice kitchen-diner through there. And look at this view.'

Shack nodded. 'It's great, baby. You did well with this one.'

She turned and smiled. 'Oh, it's not mine. It's yours.'

'What? Mine?'

She slid open the big windows, then took his hand and led him out onto the balcony. 'Well it will be, if you want it. Your client, Stella Davison, got in touch and said it was available. Soon as I saw it, I thought it would be perfect for you. This is a great location and a great price. And your office is just over there, on the other side of the quay.'

He raised her hand to his lips and kissed her fingers. 'You are some woman, Ruby Brennan. Some woman.'

'So you like it?'

'Of course I do. It's great, baby. But I'm surprise it's not been snapped up already.'

'Err . . . well it probably would have been, but I put a fifteen-grand retainer on it.'

'You did that for me?'

'Well . . . to be honest, it was your money I used.'

'My money?'

She reached up and put her arms around his neck. 'The money you left each time we made love . . . I told you I never wanted it . . . so I kept it for you . . . and that's what I used to secure this place.'

He shook his head, then laughed. 'Oh, yeah. You really are some woman.'

Chapter Fifty Two
'Six Weeks Later'

In his new apartment Shack smiled as he watched the programme intro, then picked up his phone and swiped the screen. 'Evening, Y'Ladyship.'

'Good evening. How are you?'

'Good, thanks. Are you watching North West WAGS?'

'Yes. I'm looking forward to seeing *Missus Brown* on the show. And our friend, *Mister Brown* of course.'

Shack laughed. 'Yeah. I'll bet he now wishes it was an affair, instead of her getting involved in a TV show about soccer players and their wives.'

'And of course, I think . . .'

'Hang on, love. There's someone at the door.' He quickly got up and looked through the spy-hole, then smiled. He opened the door, the smile still present. 'Hi, gorgeous. What're you doing here?'

Ruby touched his cheek as she entered. In the centre of the room she turned and said, 'It occurred to me that you haven't had a house-warming yet. So, I thought we could have one now?' She smiled at his puzzled look.

'What? At this time of night?'

She unfastened her coat and let it drop to the floor. Apart from her shoes, she was beautifully naked. 'How about we start in the bedroom?'

Shack put the phone to his ear. 'Err . . . I'll have to give you a bell in the morning. Something's just come up.'

He heard Amanda's chuckle. 'I'll bet it has . . . Give my love to Ruby.'

'Yeah, sure.'

'Good night, partner.'

'Night, Y'Ladyship.'

EPILOGUE

In the weeks and months that followed -

Maria Krol was found guilty of attempted murder. The fact that her mother and father would have been killed, had she not carried out The Red Queen's orders, had no bearing on her sentence.

Justice Andrea McDonald did however note the reasons behind the shooting of Shackleton Blister. In her summation, the judge recognised the predicament Miss Krol had found herself in and understood her actions were in no way premeditated on her part.

That said, justice must be seen to be done and Maria was still sentenced to twelve years imprisonment.

Sir Anthony Fairfax was tried for conspiracy, corruption, and accessory to murder. Despite the overwhelming evidence and the guilty verdict, he continued to profess his innocence to the very end. There were cheers from the public gallery when the twenty-five year sentenced was announced.

Throughout and after the trial, the media made great note of the disgraced civil servant's attitude and arrogance. At every opportunity, during the three weeks at the Old Bailey, Fairfax had professed his innocence. Even as he was taken from the dock he could still be heard muttering, 'I'm innocent, I'm innocent, I'm innocent.'

The Turzo brothers each received life sentences for the murder of Samantha Osbourne.

A further twenty-five years were given, for conspiracy and accessory to murder, to run concurrently.

As they climbed into the G4 Security van, to take them to prison, their gaze fell on the attractive and somewhat buxom driver. Leon leaned close to his brother, and said, 'I would.'

Milosh nodded. 'So would I.'

Sofia Novak evaded arrest in a souped-up Porsche, stolen from the Ealing film studio. The hundred and forty mile an hour car chase, along the M40, involved multiple police vehicles and two helicopters. It was only when a Rumanian truck jack-knifed at Junction 6 did the pursuit come to an horrific end. Despite Novak's considerable skill, she was unable to avoid smashing into the stationary truck. The resulting fireball could be seen over two miles away.

The Red Queen spent several weeks at Sergei Borodin's dacha, until boredom got the better of her. She left on Christmas Eve, to go to Midnight Mass. She never returned. Her whereabouts are currently unknown.

Chalky White finished his year as an *invisible man* on the streets of London and returned to his regiment at Hereford. Taking up his old position, Captain Charles

Whitehead was given a commendation for his part in Operation Hobo and awarded the Distinguished Service Cross for gallantry. Unfortunately, no one except the Home Secretary and Charles's Commanding Officer, knew about it. His friendship with Shackleton Blister would continue.

Thomas Morrison left his position as Deputy Commander, National Crime Agency. He was appointed Director in Charge, of the newly formed Oversight Committee on Police Internal Affairs. His friendship with Shackleton Blister would continue.

For her considerable contribution to the success of Operation Overwatch, Samantha Osbourne was posthumously awarded the George Cross. This being the highest civilian honour possible in Britain. A small ceremony, in Buckingham Palace, was attended by the Home Secretary; Thomas Morrison; Shack and Ruby. The Princess Royal spoke kindly to Amanda, as she pinned on the decoration.

It only took Amanda a mere seven weeks to write the book. It had it all, murder; conspiracy; money laundering and drugs. Organised-crime in bed, literally, with corrupt government officials, and bent cops from London to Leeds. Within days of its completion, she was offered deals from three major publishing houses. A week after publication her agent called to say, *The Price of Justice*, had made the UK's best seller list. She was even more delighted when asked to meet with a representative from *Netflix,* to discuss a mini-series for TV. Shack and Ruby had gone down to London to sit in on the meeting. Afterwards, the three celebrated at the *Ritz Hotel;* the bill for champagne was, to say the least, excessive.

Shack and Ruby? Well . . . who knows?

THE END